John Strange Winter

The Truth-tellers

A Novel

John Strange Winter

The Truth-tellers
A Novel

ISBN/EAN: 9783337001681

Printed in Europe, USA, Canada, Australia, Japan

Cover: Foto ©Andreas Hilbeck / pixelio.de

More available books at **www.hansebooks.com**

CONTENTS.

CHAPTER I.

OF THE NATURE OF A BOMB-SHELL . . . . . .   PAGE 9

CHAPTER II.

MISS MORTIMER LOOKS FORWARD WITH DREAD AND BACK-
WARD WITH DISMAY 21

CHAPTER III.

THE ARRIVAL OF THE TRUTH-TELLERS 29

CHAPTER IV.

ERNESTINE LEARNS SOMETHING 40

CHAPTER V.

SOME OF THE INCONVENIENCES OF TRUTH-TELLING . . . 50

CHAPTER VI.

THE GRAVITY OF BEING THE ELDEST 62

1*

CHAPTER VII.

THE INCIDENT OF THE HURDY-GURDY MAN 70

CHAPTER VIII.

TOO MUCH OF A GOOD THING 83

CHAPTER IX.

THE BREAKING OUT OF TAMMAS 90

CHAPTER X.

THE MEMORY OF A SERMON! 106

CHAPTER XI.

THE INCONVENIENCE OF GOOD INTENTIONS 121

CHAPTER XII.

A HINT OF DANGER AHEAD 134

CHAPTER XIII.

A TINGE OF WORLDLINESS 147

CHAPTER XIV.

HONOR FEELS DEEP SHAME 161

CHAPTER XV.

THE BITTER RECOGNITION OF WORLDLINESS 173

CHAPTER XVI.

A VISIT WITH A PURPOSE 180

CHAPTER XVII.

PAGE

CLEARING THE WAY 192

CHAPTER XVIII.

LIKE A TOAD UNDER A HARROW 197

CHAPTER XIX.

THE REAL AND THE WOULD-BE 208

CHAPTER XX.

HONOR MAKES A DISCOVERY 218

CHAPTER XXI.

SOME NEWS MAKES ALL THE DIFFERENCE 232

CHAPTER XXII.

NOTHING LIKE DINNER FOR HEART-BREAK 242

CHAPTER XXIII.

THE DOUBTFUL ADVANTAGES OF DECEPTION 252

CHAPTER XXIV.

WHAT IS DONE CANNOT BE UNDONE 262

CHAPTER XXV.

THE PLAIN TRUTH IS THE PLAIN TRUTH 271

THE TRUTH-TELLERS.

PART I.

CHAPTER I.

OF THE NATURE OF A BOMB-SHELL.

MISS MORTIMER came leisurely down the broad and handsome staircase of her London house, which was one of the pleasantest in that delightful old spot which is almost rebuilt now and which we call Hans Place. Miss Mortimer's house was one of the newly built ones, a handsome, red-brick mansion as to the outside, a spacious, roomy, and elegant abode as to its interior. The time was dull November. Outside, the air was thick and heavy with fog; within, Miss Mortimer's careful servants had turned up the electric light, and as she came down the spacious stairway she was greeted by the rich glow of a blazing fire which illumined the hall.

"A dreadful morning, James," she remarked, as she passed into the beautiful dining-room.

"It is, ma'am. I think we're going to 'ave a thoroughly foggy day," was James' sedate reply.

James had been many years in the employment of
Miss Mortimer, and really knew her affairs much
better than she knew them herself. " Shall you be
going out of doors to-day, ma'am ?" he enquired, as
he tucked his mistress comfortably into her accustomed place at table.

"No, James, I think not," said Miss Mortimer,
with a shuddering glance at the window, " I think
not. Yes, I will have some of that kedgeree."

The sedate James went, with the regular and careful walk of the well-trained London servant, to the
end of the table where the kedgeree was placed. He
helped his mistress to a goodly quantity, which he
placed in front of her. " A little toast, ma'am ?"

" Yes. Thank you, James. How very late the
post is this morning," Miss Mortimer added.

" I daresay it is the fog, ma'am," said James, with
an admirable mingling of indifference and regret in
his tones. " Then I may tell Cox that you will not
require anything to-day ?"

" Yes, except this evening, James. I dine at Mrs.
Halliburton's."

" Very good, ma'am. At what time ?"

" Oh—I think at a quarter to eight. But you
might look at the invitation rack."

" I will, ma'am."

He departed out of the room with the same
stealthy and catlike tread, and Miss Mortimer picked

up one of several papers which were lying on the little table set at her left hand. The first paper that she happened to take up was *Truth*, and she set it up against the coffee-pot and glanced down its pungent pages with what was evidently considerable mental refreshment. " Dear me! *Truth* gets more scurrilous every day," her thoughts ran. She had finished the kedgeree and helped herself to a kidney before the faithful James again made his appearance. This time he carried a silver tray on which were a handful of letters. "Oh, the letters at last!" said Miss Mortimer. " Thank you, James, thank you."

She opened them as they came, not taking the trouble, as some ladies do, to scrutinize the envelopes before she began her correspondence. Two invitations, three small accounts, a letter from her dressmaker asking her to be fitted on the following morning, a letter from her hair-dresser saying that he had received his fresh supplies from Paris and was now prepared to tint her hair according to her instructions, three letters from intimate friends out of London, three communications from gentlemen connected with public companies, who were most anxious to increase Miss Mortimer's income by twenty per cent., and last of all a long official-looking envelope bearing a North British postmark.

" Oh! This is from Tom. Yet that is not Tom's writing," Miss Mortimer exclaimed aloud. " Still,

that is his postmark. Ah! dear, dear; I wonder if
I shall ever get to that enchanted island of his! I
fancy not. It must be very charming living in a
feudal atmosphere, very primitive and all that kind
of thing, but five hours of open sea in what he is
pleased to call a tug—dear, dear, dear; I don't think
I can face it! One would feel such a wreck when
one landed."

She broke the seal of the letter and carelessly drew
out the contents. The first glance showed her that
it was not from her brother, but from his solicitors,
in fact. It was dated a couple of days back, and was
written from a town at one of the most northerly
points of the Scottish coasts.

"Dear Madam," it began, "we regret to inform
you of the unexpected demise of your respected
brother, Sir Thomas Mortimer, which took place at
his residence in Fynlan early yesterday morning.
Sir Thomas paid us a visit not more than a fortnight
ago, when he then seemed in the very best of health.
To us his demise was therefore quite unexpected;
but we learn from Miss Mortimer, and also from the
bailiff of the estate, that Sir Thomas had been seriously ill for several days,—in short, he died of pneu-
monia, which attacked him in an exceedingly aggra-
vated form. The late Sir Thomas's will is in our
possession, and was drawn up by us about two years

ago in accordance with his instructions. By it you are left sole guardian of his children, five in number. There will be ample provision for Sir Thomas' sons and daughters. The will is a rather complicated one, and in case you are not prepared to make so long a journey at this time of year, we are at the present moment engaged in drafting a copy of it, which we shall have the pleasure of forwarding to you as soon as completed. Our Mr. McTavish returned to Fynlan by the yacht which brought the news of Sir Thomas's demise, and it will immediately return here in order to be at your disposal in case you should wish to go to Fynlan Castle. Might we ask you to be good enough to apprise us by telegram of your intentions in this respect, and whether, in the event of your not wishing to make the journey, you will give us the necessary instructions for carrying out the late Sir Thomas's obsequies.

" We beg to remain, Madam,

" Your obedient servants,

" McGregor & McTavish."

Miss Mortimer dropped the letter upon the table and sat back in her chair with a feeling as if the end of the world had come upon her. So Thomas was dead, bluff, good-natured, crochetty, cranky Sir Thomas Mortimer, of whom she knew next to nothing, and who had left her the sole guardian of

his five children, only one of whom had she ever
seen. It was a tragedy, and Miss Mortimer drew a
long breath as she realized it! Fynlan—yes, that
was the name of the place in which he had lived and
wherein he had brought up his five children—Fynlan, and Fynlan was five hours' journey from the
most northerly point to which British land ran!
Probably they were young savages! She fancied the
eldest girl must be about sixteen; of the younger
ones she had no record. She had only seen her
sister-in-law, Lady Muriel, twice in her life; once
was when she and Sir Thomas paid a brief visit to
London, when Sir Thomas had persisted in going
about in the half-naked and wholly indecent dress of
a Highland chieftain. She remembered that he had
been rather offended because she had told him that
it was out of keeping for Sir Thomas Mortimer, a
respectable Berkshire baronet, to be making a
travesty of himself in a garb to which he had no
national rights. At all times, Sir Thomas, who was
much her senior, very much her senior, Miss Mortimer reminded herself, had been an individual of a
somewhat peppery nature, and he had been so angry
on that occasion that the poor lady had felt more
than thankful that a convenient godmother had
amply provided for all her needs, so that she was not
in the smallest degree dependent upon the favour
or kindness of her own people. Of course, she had

had a provision of five thousand pounds under her
father's will, but the interest on five thousand pounds
will not buy houses in Hans Place nor do much
towards keeping them up. Miss Mortimer's godmother had left her so exceedingly well provided for
that she was enabled, with the frankness which
wants nothing, to give any opinion which crossed
her mind without fear of disastrous consequences.
The consequences in this instance had been that she
and her sister-in-law had never become intimate;
indeed, after that short visit, she never saw Lady
Muriel but once again; that was when they had been
down to the Chase for a few days. The Chase was
the name of the old place in Berkshire which had
called the Mortimers lords for several hundreds of
years. Miss Mortimer had stayed three days with
her brother and his wife at the old house, and, looking back, she recalled how Lady Muriel had com-
plained of feeling choked and hemmed in there.

"I am not a very strong woman," she remarked,
"and I am always better in a brisk and bracing
climate. This soft Berkshire air suffocates me. I
don't think I shall ever come to the Chase again."

Poor lady, she never did go to the Chase again,
and some years afterwards, when Miss Mortimer
heard of her death, she wrote very kindly and sym-
pathetically to her brother, but she happened unfortunately to say that probably now he would be more

at the Chase and that she would see more of him. In
reply to this well-meant consolatory epistle she received an indignant and somewhat incoherent letter,
saying that he should never again visit a place which
had been disliked so much by his dear wife. " I
shall spend the rest of my life," Sir Thomas wrote,
" within sight of my darling's grave, and I shall endeavour to bring up my children on those broad and
unyielding lines of truth which were the guiding
motive of her life. At any time, my dear sister and
last living relative of my own generation, that you
care to travel so far as this lonely island you will
receive a warm and brotherly welcome ; but I do not
think I shall ever come to England again."

Years had gone by since that day, and Sir Thomas
never had travelled so far as England again. No,
he had passed his life and he had died in the island
home which he had made for himself, and Miss Mortimer wept a little—quite decorous and well-restrained
tears—to think that her only brother had passed
away without having once seen her again. " It is
very sad," she said to herself, and then she wondered
whether she had not better order the brougham in
spite of the fog, and go and consult Madame Zareen
as to the mourning which would be necessary for her
to wear.

The stately James came into the room again just
as she rose from the table. " Oh, James," said Miss

Mortimer, "I have had such dreadful news! My brother, Sir Thomas, died three days ago at his place in—that is, off that island that he lived at in Scotland.   And, James," she added, barely giving him time to do more than begin a murmur of respectful sympathy, "Sir Thomas has left me guardian, *sole* guardian of all his children.   I cannot think what we shall do with them."

"Dear me, ma'am, that is a great responsibility for you," said James.   "Where did Sir Thomas live ?"

"Oh, he lived on an island five hours' journey from—six hundred miles off," said Miss Mortimer, helplessly.

"And you will find it necessary to attend the funeral, ma'am ?"

"Oh, no, James, not this weather!   No, James; five hours of open sea in a small steam-yacht, which I expect is little more than a tug, at this time of year, is beyond me," said Miss Mortimer, with considerable emphasis; "and it is not as if I could do my poor brother any good by going.   No, I will send a telegram to the lawyers at once, authorizing them to carry out all the necessary ceremonies without me. And should you think a wreath would travel as far, James ?"

"Not a wreath of 'ot-'ouse flowers, ma'am," said James, promptly.

b   2*

"Then what ought I to do? Could I send immortelles? Would immortelles be out of keeping, do you think, James? Now, if my brother had been a soldier or a sailor, or anything of that kind, I should have sent a laurel wreath,—that would have been most appropriate,—but I cannot very well send a laurel wreath under the circumstances. Really, James, I don't know what to do. What do you think I ought to do for the best?"

"I should say, ma'am," said James, sedately, "that the florist would be the best person to advise you. Considering the time of year, ma'am, and the distance the remembrance would have to travel, I should say that they would be able to make something more appropriate than 'ot-'ouse flowers, or even a laurel wreath,—something in winter berries."

"Not mistletoe, James," said Miss Mortimer, quickly.

James coughed discreetly behind his hand. "I was not thinking of mistletoe, ma'am," he replied, quickly, "but 'olly berries, 'olly berries and other things of a similar nature would look a little cheerful at this time of year, don't you think, ma'am? And they would travel well."

"Well, James, I think if you can send round to Cox and get him to bring me the brougham at once, —I really don't like taking the horses out this weather, to say nothing of poor Cox,—but it is imperative that I should have my mourning. You can explain the circumstances to him."

"Very good, ma'am," said James, blandly. "Then might I ask, ma'am, shall you be goin' up at all ?"

"Not this time of year, James, certainly not. It would be as much as my life was worth; and as I am left these children's sole guardian I must regard my own as a more valuable life than I have done up to now. I cannot think what I shall do with them," she added, looking helplessly round as if she was considering whether she could put up five beds in different corners of the room. "I suppose there are schools and things to be had. You see, James, we are not accustomed to young people."

"They will make the 'ouse bright and lively, ma'am," said James, who was great at making the best of things. "It will give you a fresh interest in life, Miss Mortimer. For my part, ma'am, I always like to 'ave young ladies and gentlemen about the 'ouse. Then shall I send off the telegram that you mentioned just now ?"

"Oh, yes, James; I had forgotten it. Wait a moment. I will write it at once."

She sat down at a writing-table which stood on one side of the spacious fireplace and addressed a telegram to McGregor & McTavish——"Quite impossible for me to make so long a journey in this weather. My health imperatively forbids it," she

wrote. " I will leave it to you to make all necessary
arrangements for my brother's funeral and for mourning for his children and servants. Carry out what
you believe would have been his own wishes, and
kindly convey my deepest sympathy to my nieces
and nephews." She signed it " Elinor Mortimer,"
and handed it to the attendant James with a deep
sigh.

CHAPTER II.

MISS MORTIMER LOOKS FORWARD WITH DREAD AND BACKWARD WITH DISMAY.

Two days later Miss Mortimer received from Mc-Gregor & McTavish the copy of her brother's last will and testament. They had indeed spoken truly when they described it as a somewhat complicated document. It was more than complicated; it was voluminous to a degree. It set forth in the usual legal phraseology that the testator was of sound mind, and that he had died in the fear of God and in the full belief of salvation to come, and then went on to dispose of his large properties, the main portion to the boy. All the Berkshire property, his several Scottish estates, and the island and castle of Fynlan were to go with the title to his eldest son, Thomas; to his younger son—apparently only two of the five children were boys—he left in strict trust for himself and his children a sum in money of fifty thousand pounds; to each of his three daughters he left in the same manner twenty-five thousand pounds. Then came a long list of possessions, some of which he wished to go with the title as heirlooms, some of which he wished to be held in trust by his sister and

executrix for the younger and other children.   Nothing was left to chance; every little thing had been
carefully thought out and arranged for.   Then he
appointed his sister, Elinor Mortimer, spinster, of
Hans Place, London, as his children's sole guardian.
He left to her a sum of five thousand pounds and a
certain necklet which had belonged to their mother
as a small return for the trouble which he was re-
luctantly compelled, by circumstances over which
she would understand he had no control, to place
upon her.   The trustees, whom he named, were to
pay over to the said Elinor Mortimer a sum of not
less than five thousand a year for the maintenance
and education of his children.   This sum was to remain unaltered so long as any of his children were
under age, but as they came of age it was to be re-
duced by one-fifth.   His daughters were not to
marry without their guardian's consent until they
were of full age, but if they married with her consent
before that time their incomes were to be paid over
on the marriage-day.   Then Sir Thomas gave at
length his reasons for having selected his sister for
this office and trust.

"My sister herself, and others whom it may or
may not concern," the testament ran, "may think it
somewhat strange that I should have placed this
great trust upon one of whom I have seen but little
during my married life.   I will briefly recount my

reasons for having made such a choice, and will also ask my sister to bear one or two things in mind, which I shall thank her to regard as my last and most earnest wishes concerning the bringing up of my dear children. My late dear wife's main principle in life was an unswerving love of truth, and, in accordance with her wishes and my own desires, I have brought up my children in what I might almost call a new religion. I care nothing for creeds, believing that only the truth will last when all else shall have faded away. King Agrippa asked, ' What is truth ?' It is to be a truth-teller; and we inhabitants of the isle of Fynlan are proud to call ourselves the truth-tellers to and before the whole world. Being fifteen years older than my sister Elinor, I have naturally not much remembrance of intimate personal intercourse with her during the days of our childhood,— we were not children at the same time,—but I have before me a very frequent remembrance of a phrase which was most often upon her lips as a little child in our old Berkshire home. ' It is the truth !' was her most frequent cry. And I have also the remembrance of a disagreement of thought which occurred during my last visit to the metropolis between my sister, my wife, and myself. This difference of thought did not lead to any difference of friendship, —at least, not upon our side,—but my sister told me that she considered I had no right to wear the High-

land costume, which has been my adopted garb ever
since I first came to live upon the island of Fynlan.
In a certain sense I did not agree with my sister, but
I have thought many times since that day that her
remark pointed to an exceedingly honourable and
upright sense of rectitude, which in reality went further in the cause of truth than even I had tried to
do. It is because I feel convinced that my only sister has an innate and inborn love of the great quality
of truthfulness that I have chosen her before the
whole world to be the guardian of my children. I
will ask her as the last request that I shall ever make—
for she will not know of this until I shall have passed
to my forefathers—to keep before her in her dealings
with my children only that one great principle, to
keep them truthful, to see that they go on as they
have begun, that they are the truth-tellers. She will
find them frank, fearless, and open to a degree.
They do not understand anything that is underhand,
—deceit is not in them. I entreat my sister in the
case of my daughters not to entrust their education
wholly to others; I mean that she shall not send
them to boarding-schools, of which my dear dead
wife had no opinion. In the case of my sons, it is,
of course, necessary that they should receive a public school education" (" For which thank God!"
ejaculated Miss Mortimer, piously). " I have a preference for Eton, but I will leave that to my sister's

wisdom and discretion. I will also leave to her, until my son comes of age, the entire use of my castle of Fynlan, and of the Chase, where we were both born, so that she may make their home where seems best to her from time to time. In all general details I would wish my children to have the education that befits their station in life. I leave to them my fondest blessings, and beg them to remember in all the circumstances of life that their mother was a woman of blameless·integrity and of stainless honour; a higher example they could not follow. Of their unworthy father I will ask them to think with leniency, remembering always that he was early bereaved of the support and comfort of a blessed companion and bright example."

Miss Mortimer laid down the copy of the will and wiped her eyes with a wisp of embroidered cambric. "Most touching, I am sure," she said, with a little gurgle in her voice. "Poor Thomas! I am sure it was a very good thing for Muriel that he saw all those virtues in her. I thought she was a detestable person. Ah, well, well, I suppose there is always some one who believes in us through thick and thin. Perhaps if she had lived—but there, it is an unworthy thought, and I will not give expression to it even in my own mind. Poor Thomas! Five children! Dear, dear, whatever shall we do with five children! I am sure if Thomas knew that I had so little real sympathy with his poor Muriel he would not have chosen me as his children's guardian. It is all very sad, very sad. Well, let me see what else he says."

She tucked the wisp of cambric into the bosom of her dress and took up the copy of the will again. It was some little time before she could find the place at which she had left off reading its contents. She had, however, mastered the greater part of its message, and she read to the end and then laid it aside with another deep sigh. " I suppose," she said to herself, " that I cannot leave these young things up there alone with only their savage servants and such like to take care of them. I once went up to pay a visit in the Highlands, not nearly as far north as Fynlan, and really they might have been Chocktaw Indians for aught I would have known to the contrary. They could not speak English, and they called everything *she*,—even the men. I wonder if my nieces and nephews will call James she! If I remember rightly, they called themselves she. I suppose I had better send for them to come down here. Dear, dear, dear, to think of five young barbarians, who have never been off their Shetland island, being suddenly shot into one's life as five separate and grave responsibilities! Oh, my dear Thomas, if only you had mixed with the world a little more, your sister Elinor is the very last person whom you would have chosen to carry out your dear Muriel's particular cranks in the way of bringing up children! I wonder whether I had better send James up to fetch them, or whether I had better let one of their Highland retainers bring them down and deliver them to me here on the doorstep. Really, I wish I had somebody whose advice I could ask. If it had been summer I could have gone up to—well, as far as McGregor & McTavish's office, and I could have awaited the arrival of that dreadful little steamer, but in this weather—the end of November, to travel six hundred miles to discuss business matters of the dryest character with gentlemen who would talk with such a Highland accent that I should not be able to make head nor tail of them, well, that is a little too trying even for poor Tom's sake—to say nothing of Muriel. Oh, dear, dear, what a misfortune to think that both Thomas and Muriel should be dead and gone, and what a greater misfortune to think that they should have left five olive branches for me to take care of. I feel really as if, well, as if life was getting too much for me! And to think that poor Thomas should be so impressed with an idea that I am afflicted with a passion for the truth. A greater mistake was never made in this world. It only shows, when you get a little twisted in your mind, how every action in life becomes subservient to the one warp. To think that the only thing that

Thomas remembers of my childhood should be a little trick I had of saying, " It is the truth!" And to think that he should put such a construction upon my very natural annoyance at his going about in London with his legs all naked and petticoats on! Oh, dear, dear, dear, what a queer world this is! And I wonder," she said, with a sudden drop of the jaw, " whether the ` young Sir Thomas and his brother will both be naked boys in petticoats, and afflicted with a passion for carrying out their father's last wishes."

PART II.

CHAPTER III.

THE ARRIVAL OF THE TRUTH-TELLERS.

IN due course of time the house in Hans Place was entirely ready for its young guests, and the day and hour of their arrival drew very near. Miss Mortimer had arrayed herself in the most becoming mourning, a little deeper, perhaps, than she would have thought necessary had the late Sir Thomas's will not rendered it necessary that his children should be transported from their Shetland home to her own immediate vicinity. Miss Mortimer was a lady who had no belief in that grief which runs rampant. Her regrets for her only brother were subdued and decorous. Left to her own unbiassed judgment, they would have taken the form of light and airy attire, and by that I do not mean light and airy as to texture, but rather as an indication of depth of woe. However, as she was so soon to expect the immediate presence of her young nieces and nephews, she sacrificed her personal inclinations sufficiently to order mourning which was really quite deep in its character.

"No, Madame Zareen, I will not begin with chif-

fon," she replied in response to a really touching
suggestion from the great dress-maker on the subject
of chiffon as an embellishment to a dinner costume;
" I will not begin with chiffon.   You see I should not
like in any way to hurt the feelings of these poor
young creatures, and although the loss of a brother
is a very great loss, yet it is not in any way commen-
surate with the terrible blank which is left by the
death of a parent,—an only remaining parent, too.
Well, perhaps, I may have just a little jet on the
sleeves, but nothing showy.   I wouldn't hurt their
poor young feelings for the world."

So, by the time the five young Shetlanders were
due in Hans Place, Miss Mortimer might have been
seen arrayed in garments which would not have done
any discredit to a widow who had just got over the
first symptoms of her grief,—I mean, who had just
changed her weeds for more every-day garments.

" Dear me, Rosine," she said, for quite the twen-
tieth time, " they ought to be here by this time."

" Ah, yes, madam," replied the French woman,
easily; " ze trains are late at this time of year, ze fog
answer for so much."

" True, true," said Miss Mortimer, " very true, Rosine, but still I wish it was over."

" I hope zat they will not cry ver' much," said
Rosine, looking out of the window.   " But there,
madam, they are young, and the young forget ver'

soon. When ze first shock is over you will have great pleasure in them, it will be like de—ear little puppy-dogs or pussy-cats. They will give you much pleasure."

" Like five young Shetland ponies," said Miss Mortimer, drily. She had none of the enthusiasm of her retainers.

" Here is ze omnibus," said Rosine, eagerly.

Miss Mortimer rose and went to the window. Yes, there was the railway 'bus with its pair of horses, and the face of faithful James showing just within the door. The top was piled with luggage, upon the pavement were two panting runners wiping their heated.brows. Before Miss Mortimer's blurred vision—for a crowd of emotions swept across her mind at the very thought of her brother's orphan children—there rose a confused kaleidoscope view of children, bare-legged tartans, dogs, cats, birds, and luggage, all revolving around the faithful James. " Oh, dear, dear, it is dreadful," said Miss Mortimer, as she hurried from the luxurious and warm morning-room out into the hall.

In two minutes they all came trooping into the house. Miss Mortimer's worse fears were realized. Barbarians? They were worse. They had not a stitch of black among the five of them! She looked down at her own sombre garments and thought how she had sacrificed herself lest she should hurt the feelings of her nieces and nephews, and they, fresh from their father's funeral, had come in all the brazen gorgeousness of a tartan that was not their own. Such a tartan! Not even quiet red and blue with a yellow bar across it like the Macdonald's and the Gordon's; no, it was an aggressive conglomeration of every vivid, gaudy, and aniline tint to be found in any scheme of colour. Before she had found any words of greeting for them, Miss Mortimer resolved upon an early visit to Madame Zareen with a view to modifying her own outward expressions of grief. Then she hurried forward and caught the first of the newcomers in her arms in token of welcome. This was evidently the eldest girl, a tall young thing just entering upon womanhood. Miss Mortimer noticed with a thrill of satisfaction that even in her hideous and barbaric garb she was as lovely as a June morning.

"So this is Aunt Elinor," she cried in a fresh, young, joyous voice. "We feel like an invading army. I am afraid we are going to be a dreadful, terrible trouble to you. You see we have never lived in a town before; we have never even seen a town before. Tom, Tom, come and speak to Aunt Elinor at once. Where are your manners?"

"So this is Tom," said Miss Mortimer, putting both her hands on the boy's shoulders and looking at him with keenest interest. She was trying to trace some likeness to father or mother, but so far she could see none to either parent. "You are Ernestine?" she said, addressing the tall girl.

"Yes, Aunt Elinor, I am Ernestine. And this is Honor—and this is Crystal—Tom here—and this is Georgie."

"Georgie? That is a very every-day, ordinary sort of name," said Miss Mortimer, who, if the truth be told, was rather dismayed by the first names of her three nieces.

"Yes. He was called George Washington, because, you know, George Washington never told lies," said Ernestine, glibly. "Our names all mean something, except Tom's; and father used to say he was called Thomas because there was a long string of Sir Thomas Mortimers before him. I believe dear mother wished to call him Bayard, but she gave way to father's racial prejudices."

By the time Miss Mortimer had kissed the five newcomers and had successfully placed their names, the panting runners had got most of the luggage within the house.

"Oh, by-the-bye, Aunt Elinor," said Ernestine, just as Miss Mortimer had opened her mouth to suggest that they might as well go into the dining-room, "those poor creatures who ran all the way from the railway station, James says that they are on the look-out for what he calls a tip. We did not

c

know what a tip was, but they ran all the way. You
are going to give them something, aren't you?"

"Oh, yes, my dear; James will see to that," said
Miss Mortimer, nervously. She had a horror of
street runners herself, for she was always rather
suspicious about her silver.

"Oh, James will see to that? What are you
going to give them, James?" asked Ernestine, turning round like a flash of morning light upon the
astonished butler.

"I suppose we shall be obliged to give them a
shilling a-piece, ma'am?" he said in an undertone to
his mistress.

"What! Do people in London run all that way
for a shilling and get no more? Don't you send
them round to the kitchen to get some food?" ejaculated Ernestine, blankly.

Miss Mortimer looked at James and groaned—in
the spirit, if not actually in reality. "No, my dear,
we do not entertain in that way in London. We do
not keep open house; it would never do. Give them
a couple of shillings each, James. I hope that will
satisfy them."

"Gawd bless you, l'ydy. It's the first money I've
earned to-day," said one of the men in a thick yet
rapturous voice. "There is people in 'ouses as big
as this wot 'll let you run for miles and then offer
you tuppence to carry in a pile of luggage bigger

nor this. Gawd bless you! You are a real l'ydy."

Then Miss Mortimer led the way into the dining-room, followed there by the troop of young people.

"And what sort of a journey had you, my dears? Are you not all longing for your tea?"

"No! No!" returned two or three fresh young voices in the same breath, "because, you see, we did mostly nothing but have tea or something all the way down. Cook made us up a hamper to last us the whole way, and Tammas brought us a spirit-lamp and kettle and a big canful of water, which he got filled at almost every station. Oh, we had a very nice journey, thank you, Aunt Elinor."

"And who is Tammas?" asked Miss Mortimer, in some bewilderment.

"Oh, Tammas is the piper. We could not go anywhere without Tammas," replied Ernestine, promptly.

"Do you mean a person who plays the bag-pipes?" asked Miss Mortimer, in a tone of absolute horror.

"Yes. Of course, nobody of position travels without a piper. We should as soon have thought of coming without—oh, without our dogs and such like as without Tammas."

"But, my dears, do you expect me to have Tam-mas living here in this house?"

THE TRUTH-TELLERS.

"Oh, we don't know about that," said Ernestine, quickly. "Of course, we don't know where you are going to arrange that *we* shall live, but we cannot live without Tammas, that's a certainty."

"Oh! And what does Tammas do? Does he make himself useful, or how?'"

"Yes, Tammas is a most handy man. He will do almost anything. He always plays when we are having dinner, and in winter he used to play in the corridor, because Fynlan is rather cold, you know, and in summer he played outside on the terrace in front of the windows. There are seven windows in the dining-room at Fynlan, so that Tammas|had a good long march up and down. Oh! It is fine to hear him skirling the bag-pipes!"

Miss Mortimer put her hand across her eyes as if trying to shut out the hideous picture thus conjured up.

"And when you have a party," Ernestine went on, "he will stand in the hall; and although you may not care to have him playing the pipes all the time, he looks well, and everybody will speak to him, of course, and everybody will pass the time of day, and you will find Tammas most useful, really, Aunt Elinor."

"We shall see," said Miss Mortimer, it must be confessed, rather doubtfully. "Now, my dears, before we settle the fate of Tammas, would you not like to come up-stairs and take your things off and wash your hands? And by that time tea will be ready."

"We'll do just as you like," said Ernestine. "Our hands are quite clean, in fact we washed them in the train just before we got off in case you came to meet us. We may as well put our things here, if you don't mind?"

She began to unwind her plaid from her shoulders as she spoke. It was a complicated and voluminous garment, and when it was all off and had been cast upon a sofa hard by, to be followed a moment later by the dark-green Tam-o'Shanter with its eagle's feather, which Ernestine had worn upon her sunny head, Miss Mortimer was able better to see what manner of young lady her eldest niece really was. And she was fain to admit that a lovelier young creature had never come across her horizon. She *was* lovely. Miss Mortimer recognized the fact with the first feeling of satisfaction which had crossed her mind during the past week, for she was tall and straight as a willow-wand, with the wonderful fair skin, purely pink and white, which goes with sunshiny hair that is not quite golden, and she had brilliant blue-gray eyes. She had a bewitching mouth, with a single dimple in the left cheek, an adorable nose, neither too large nor too small, rather a long throat, and a voice which had not the faintest trace of a northern accent.

4

" How is it," said Miss Mortimer, as she drew her chair to the table, " that you children have lived all your lives in the wilds of—Scotland——"

" But we have *not* lived in Scotland," said Ernestine, quickly. " Fynlan is not Scotland."

" Well, dear, in the wilds of Fynlan—and that you have not got the faintest trace of a Scotch accent ?"

" I don't know," said Ernestine, almost blankly.

" I have only been once to the Highlands," said Miss Mortimer, " in my life, but I was struck then with the terrible way in which people spoke. The people all called everything *she*,—even the men, and a man will speak of himself as ' she will do so-and-so.' "

" Oh, yes," said Ernestine. " But those are just Highlanders ; I suppose they would talk like that, but our people speak only Gaelic; they do not understand English at all."

" And Tammas, doesn't Tammas speak or understand English ?"

" Well—only such English as he has picked up from us. How should he ? He has never seen an ordinary English person in his life excepting ourselves, and we speak Gaelic exactly as we speak English. We always had a French and German governess, and our father and mother spoke English as you do. We had no chance of learning to speak broken English."

"Oh, I see. Ah! Well, that simplifies matters very much," said Miss Mortimer, "very much, indeed. I am quite relieved that you do talk as you do."

"Georgie," said Ernestine, suddenly, at that moment, "I don't think you had better take any more of that. You know it always gives you the stomach-ache."

CHAPTER IV.

ERNESTINE LEARNS SOMETHING.

WHEN Miss Mortimer perceived the kind of tea of which her nieces and nephews disposed on their arrival in Hans Place, she thought, with something like dismay, that her general table would have to be very much altered from that time forward. "Of course," her thoughts ran, "it would be easy to un- derstand that five healthy young people should eat like cormorants on just coming off a long journey;" but then they had been at pains to impress her with the fact that they had been amply provisioned from the time of their leaving Fynlan Castle, and also that Tammas had procured them fresh water at every stopping-place of importance.

"I must have a talk with cook first thing in the morning," she said to herself when she was alone for a minute or so. "I expect she will be leaving,— cooks are very queer creatures,—and a cook who has been accustomed to a small and dainty appetite will take very badly to having to provide for five cormo- rants."

She was aroused from these thoughts by the en- trance of Ernestine. "I thought you would like to

know, Aunt Elinor," she began, "that the children
are quite settled down in their own sitting-room.
What a dear little house yours is!"

The words gave Miss Mortimer somewhat of a
shock. She was not accustomed to regard her house
as a little house. "I expect, my dear, that Fynlan
Castle is very large?"

"Well, we never thought so," said Ernestine, without hesitation; "but compared with this it is an immense place. I suppose living in towns you get
used to being cooped up all higgledy-piggledy."

"Well, dear, of course, when I bought this house,"
said Miss Mortimer, with dignity, "it was intended
only for myself, not for a family of young people."

"Ah, I see; yes. But father always said that
town houses were very small compared with country
places. I suppose you like this better than a house
like the castle?"

"I have never seen the castle, my dear," said Miss
Mortimer, gently; "it is such a long journey. I
always meant to come, but somehow I never accom-
plished it. I want you, whilst we are alone,—I mean
while we are without the younger ones,—to tell me
all about your dear father's death. It was very sad;
it was a great shock to me."

"Yes, so it was to us," said Ernestine, in the most
matter-of-fact tone; "so it was to us. We had always looked upon father as somebody who never got

ill. It was very strange that he should find just a
cold too much for him as he did. I don't understand
it; but you know I think father took the right view
himself."

"And what view was that?" asked Miss Mortimer,
holding a hand-screen between herself and the fire.

"Well, he had been out all the day,—I don't quite
know what he had been doing; but he came in, and
I was sitting reading in the hall. 'Hullo, father!' I
said. He looked at me in a queer sort of way, and
he sat down on the big settle by the fire. 'Ernestine,'
he said, 'I have got my death-blow.' 'Good gracious, father,' I said, 'what is that?' 'I mean that I
am going to be very ill, and ten chances to one I
shall not get over it.' I didn't believe him, you
know, Aunt Elinor. I thought he was frightened or
feeling very bad, and I advised him to go to bed, and
we sent for the doctor; but four days after father
was gone. Oh, it was dreadfully sudden!"

"I am sure it must have been a terrible shock to
you," said Miss Mortimer. "I know that it was to
me. Indeed, my dear, I can hardly realize it. To
think that poor Thomas, whom I had always re-
garded as so strong, and hale, and hearty, should
have been cut off really in his very prime. It is very
sad, very sad! But, my dear, there is one thing I
should like to say to you while we are together and
alone—you travelled down in your ordinary clothes?"

"Why, yes. Would you have worn your best things for a journey?" asked Ernestine.

"No, my dear, certainly not. I think it was most prudent of you to consider your wardrobes, but, of course, it is a little unusual, so soon after a funeral—so soon after a bereavement—to be wearing colours."

"But we have nothing else," said Ernestine.

"Nothing else?" said Miss Mortimer, sharply. "You don't mean to say that all your clothing is like that?"

"Yes; we never wore anything else—any of us."

"Do you mean to tell me," said Miss Mortimer, "that you have no mourning?"

"We have bands round our arms," said Ernestine, simply, pointing to a deep band of crape which encircled the upper part of her left sleeve.

"But, my dear Ernestine," cried Miss Mortimer, blankly, "it is positively indecent for children, whose only surviving parent is taken away from them, to wear colours."

"No, not colours. This is our tartan."

"But you have no tartan," cried Miss Mortimer. "You are not Scotch people. That tartan is not yours. It is not as if you were Macdonalds or Gordons or Stuarts, or anything of that kind."

Ernestine looked at her aunt with her beautiful, frank eyes. "But this is our tartan, Aunt Elinor," she said, simply. "You forget that the tartan goes with the place."

"Then, my dear," said Miss Mortimer, with the nearest approach to severity that she could assume, "then, my dear, that tartan should stay with the place. What you choose to wear when you are in the wilds of the Shetland Isles——"

"Do you mean Fynlan?" asked Ernestine.

"Yes, my dear, I mean that—that—island where you have lived all your lives—what you choose to wear when you are there is one thing, but what you wear when you are in civilized London is quite another matter altogether. That is the first thing I must ask you to do for me. To-morrow morning I will take you all and have you properly and suitably dressed in mourning, proper mourning, such as other people wear. Look at me."

"You look so dull," said Ernestine, in a very dissatisfied tone.

Miss Mortimer bit her lips. "Yes, I am wearing rather deep mourning. I ordered it a little deeper than I should have had it in the ordinary course of events—wholly and solely upon your account, my dear."

"But why upon our account? We have never worn mourning in our lives."

"Not when your mother died?"

"No. We wore bands round our arms."

" And your father wished that?"

" Yes, I imagine so."

" Well, that may be the custom of Fynlan, but I am quite sure that your father would wish you to conform to the customs of every-day London life while you are living with me in London."

" Then you are not going back to Fynlan with us ?" said Ernestine, in rather a crestfallen tone.

" I have no such intention—at present," said Miss Mortimer, guardedly. " The state of my health would not allow me to live in so bleak a place. Next summer we will perhaps go up there for our holidays."

" Oh! And don't you mean to take us back to Fynlan till next summer?" Ernestine cried.

" I think not," said Miss Mortimer, " I think not."

" Oh, well, I daresay we shall be very happy here," said Ernestine, in a tone which implied that they would make the best of the situation. " I am sure I hope we shall not be very much trouble to you. You must tell us when we do things that you don't like ; but, of course, you will do that in any case. As for the mourning, why, Aunt Elinor, we will do anything that you like, and we will wear what you tell us. We have no prejudices to speak of; father always used to say we were a singularly unprejudiced family. Now, you know, nobody could say that about father, for if ever a prejudiced human

being trod the earth, poor, dear father was that one.
Don't you agree with me?"

It is safe to say that the soul of Miss Mortimer
turned positively sick within her. Assuredly. there
was no deceit in these young people. Poor Sir
Thomas had been right in that. She passed over
Ernestine's criticism of her so lately dead and gone
father without remark. "Then, dear, we will consider that settled, and to-morrow I will see that you
all have clothing suitable to wear for London. If it
pleases you, you can wear your plaid things when we
go back to Fynlan."

"You mean our tartans," said Ernestine, simply.

"Dear Ernestine," said Miss Mortimer, "I—I—
don't like to find fault with you so soon, but there is
one thing I should like very much just to point out."
Poor lady, she was getting quite nervous, but Ernestine fixed her with her bright eyes and said,—

"What is it, auntie? Speak out."

"Well, dear, you said to Georgie at tea that he
was not to eat any of that *foie gras*, because it always
gave him the stomach-ache."

"So it does," said Ernestine, promptly. "He
knows that as well as I do."

"Yes, dear, I have no doubt. It was very kind
and sisterly of you to warn the dear child, but James
was in the room."

"But, dear Aunt Elinor, James being in the room

would not stop Georgie from having a stomach-ache, would it?"

"No, my dear, but you might have put it in a different way?"

"I don't understand you," said Ernestine.

"Well, dear, for a young lady of your age and position to—to—to—talk of the stomach-ache before a man-servant—er—well, it is not quite the right thing."

"But why isn't it the right thing?"

"Ernestine, my dear, did your governesses never tell you such matters?"

"No."

"But you had French and German governesses, you told me."

"Of course we had."

"And did they never tell you that a young lady would not dream of speaking of her stomach before a man-servant—before anybody except her doctor?"

"No, certainly not," said Ernestine. "Of course, it is our stomach, isn't it? What else was I to say? I couldn't say it would give him a headache."

"No, dear; but you might have said it would make him feel a little ill, or that it would disagree with him."

"Oh, I see! You mean it is not polite to speak of your stomach?"

"Exactly so."

"Oh, very well, Aunt Elinor, I won't do it, of course not. We don't wish to make ourselves nuisances to you. You see, poor dear father had rather a craze about always telling the truth ; sometimes it was a little inconvenient, but he always declared that he never minded the inconvenience so long as we told the bare truth. But as to that, dear, we will do exactly as you wish ; you must only tell us when there is anything that you don't quite like, because, you know, we have been brought up entirely on father's principles, and, of course, as sometimes I have said to him, he was not the only person in the world, and one wants to live so as to please the greatest number of people. Of course, as long as father lived, it was all very well, and we were quite content to please him, but now we have got to live with you, we would prefer to please you. That is only right and proper, isn't it ?"

"Well, dear, I hope," said Miss Mortimer, in rather a choking voice, for the girl's evident desire to please her touched her deeply, " I hope, dear, that we shall not either of us find it very difficult. We must bear with each other, and pray let us keep in mind that you will wish to do nothing and I shall ask you to do nothing that would really go against your father's principles. Of course, the truth is a very beautiful and a very precious quality, but it is not always expedient to tell the exact truth,—I mean,

it is not always expedient to say just what comes
into your mind, to say what happens to be true ; and
in England, in London, among people of social position, young ladies in particular are a little careful as
to what parts of the human body they speak of
Stomachs are not mentioned except in church, dear.
Of course, many things in church are mentioned that
one takes in a particular way. At dinner-tables,
one's stomach is never spoken of."

PART III.

CHAPTER V.

SOME OF THE INCONVENIENCES OF TRUTH-TELLING.

MISS MORTIMER had for years past been at home to her friends once a fortnight, second and fourth Tuesdays were her reception days, and, like many other well-to-do ladies in London, she was somewhat particular not to receive stray visitors who chose to call at other times. The faithful James knew those who were honored by having what might be called the perpetual *entrée* to his mistress's presence; they were not many, although Miss Mortimer's general acquaintance was a very large one.

It happened the very day after the arrival of the young Mortimers in London that the two younger girls, Honor and Crystal, were passing through the hall from the upper part of the house to the morning-room. They reached the front door just in time to hear a very smart lady, who had got out of a very smart single brougham, inquire of the faithful James whether Miss Mortimer was at home.

" Not at 'ome, ma'am," James replied, in the peculiarly urbane manner of a good servant who knows particularly well that his mistress is at that moment toasting her toes upon the bar of her boudoir fender.

The elder of the two young ladies from the wilds of Fynlan never hesitated for a moment, but went forward, saying, in her clear and exceedingly well-bred voice, "Oh, you are quite mistaken, James. My aunt is at home."

"I think not, Miss 'Onor," replied James, blandly.

"Indeed, I have just come from the boudoir. She is sitting there now," said Honor, a little indignantly.

"I am sure I beg your pardon, Miss 'Onor. I quite thought Miss Mortimer 'ad gone out. This way, if you please, ma'am," he said, turning to the visitor.

His manner was so admirable that the lady was quite deceived, and followed him into the house, as she certainly would not have done if she had realized that Miss Mortimer was not that day receiving. The faithful James was, however, much too good a servant to usher the lady into the drawing-room, and so convey to her that she had been admitted by the purest accident. He escorted her straight to the boudoir and announced her as if it was indeed his mistress's ordinary custom to receive on that day and in that place, and in five minutes' time he carried up tea, as if the visitor had come by a special invitation, and was one for whom he was particularly prepared.

It happened that this particular lady was one of

Miss Mortimer's especial dislikes, and she took James pretty severely to task when her caller had departed. "James," she said, quite sharply, "whatever induced you to bring Mrs. de Vallincourt in as if she was my most intimate friend? Why, I scarcely know her."

James coughed deprecatingly behind his hand.
"Well, ma'am," he replied, apologetically, "I was very awkwardly situated. I really had no choice, ma'am."

"But why?"

"Well, ma'am, Mrs. de Vallincourt asked if you was at 'ome, and I said not; but two of the young ladies was passing through the 'all at the moment, and Miss 'Onor she up and said, without a moment's hesitation, 'You are quite mistaken; James; my aunt is in the boudoir.' I told Miss 'Onor that I thought you was not at 'ome, but as she said she 'ad just come down from the boudoir and 'ad left you there, I 'ad no choice but to bring the lady in."

"Oh, dear me!" said Miss Mortimer, with a sigh; "I shall have to make such an explanation about being at home and not at home! Really, I beg your pardon, James. I thought it was very strange that you should make such a mistake."

Accordingly, Miss Mortimer took the first chance of explaining to her two young nieces that they must not interfere with old and valuable servants like the faithful James. "You see, my darlings," she said, trying hard to be most kind and motherly, so as not to frighten the dear children as she put it in her own mind, " London is not like Fynlan; it is a very large place, dears, and nothing could be more inconvenient than having a great crowd of friends dropping in at any time of the day that they thought fit. So, as it is considered very rude to say that one is engaged if one cannot conveniently receive one's friends, it is the regular custom for good servants to say ' not at home.' "

" But if you say not at home when you are," said Honor, doughtily, " that is not telling the truth."

" Well, dear, that lady who called this afternoon would not have asked ; she would not have thought or troubled as to whether I was really in the house or not. It is a mere form, but it has been found to be the most convenient form that there is. Possibly she only called as a duty because she dined here a few nights ago, and she would have been as glad to get off coming in as I would have been glad not to receive her. People who have a very large acquaint- ance, who have to make calls out of pure politeness, are very frequently most grateful when they find their friends not at home. Don't you under- stand ?"

" No," said Honor ; " I don't understand at all. It seems to me that if a person asks if you are in, if you are at home and you say you are not when you are, that is telling a lie. That is what we should call it in Fynlan, anyway."

" My dear, I don't suppose that you had any callers in Fynlan."

" Oh, yes, we had. There was the doctor's wife and there was the minister's wife; they called sometimes, and then people would come over from the other islands, but then, of course, they always came to lunch or to dinner, or to stay the night or something, but still, we would not have said we were out when we were actually in."

" No, dear; but if you were living in London you would do as other people do. A phrase like not at home is not a lie when it is intended to deceive,—it is a mere conventionality."

" James knew you were in and he said you were not in, and that poor lady would have gone away if it hadn't been for me."

" Yes, dear, she would, and probably she would not thank you for wasting her time when leaving a card would have answered the same purpose."

" I call that hypocrisy," said Honor.

" Well, dear, you are very young and you don't understand the ways of the world yet, and, at all events, I must ask you not, under any circumstances, to interfere with James, because he is a very valuable servant who understands his work, and you know, dear, servants cannot bear to be interfered with."

"I didn't mean to interfere," said Honor; "why should I? I thought James would be glad to know you were in. I thought he thought you were out."

"Not at all, dear. James understands and you don't. Now we quite understand each other, don't we?"

"Oh, yes, Aunt Elinor," said Honor, promptly. "I will leave James to tell what lies he likes another time."

"Not lies, my dear," said Miss Mortimer, with gentle persistence.

"You may call them what you like, Aunt Elinor," said Honor, sturdily, "but you cannot make anything else of it. It *was* a lie, and a thumping one! I know," she went on, in a tone of unshaken conviction, "that if father had caught one of our people telling such a down-right lie as that he would have sent him out of the house on the spot. Father could not bear lies."

In her distress and dismay Miss Mortimer appealed to Ernestine. "Ernestine, my dear," she said, "it seems to me that you are the only one of your brothers and sisters who in any way understands me," and then she related to her eldest niece her little difficulty regarding Honor.

Ernestine put the matter in a nut-shell. "Look here, Honor," she said, brusquely enough, to her sister, "when you were at home at Fynlan, you did as father did and what he wanted, and when you are living in Hans Place you have got to do what auntie wants, so don't you get interfering with James. If James tells stories to please auntie, it is part of his duty, and you are not responsible."

" But it is not the truth," said Honor, making a last gallant effort to prove herself in the right.

" Never mind about the truth," said Ernestine; " truth was father's pet fad, and it is all very well in Fynlan, but we are not in Fynlan now; we are in Hans Place. You have got to do in Hans Place what other people do or else you are out of it, so don't let us hear any more about whether James tells the truth or not, or else we shall have to send you back to Fynlan to tell the truth there. Really, Honor, it is very stupid of you ! For mercy's sake, don't let us have any more of it !"

· She hustled her young sister out of the room and came back to the fireplace with the evident view of smoothing down Miss Mortimer's ruffled feathers. " Dear Aunt Elinor," she said, putting her slim young arm protectingly about Miss Mortimer's shoulders, " I am afraid we are a dreadful trouble to you. I will speak to James, and tell him that he must not mind the children's little ways till they get more used to London life. I remember once, dear, the minister at Fynlan telling father that his ideas would not work in every-day life, and father was so

angry with him. But they don't, you know, Aunt
Elinor. Mr. Duncan was quite right. You see,
when a visitor came to the castle it was quite an
occasion with us. We used to wear our best tartans, and fraulein and mademoiselle used to put on
their best dresses, and we would be cooking and
putting out fresh flowers and making no end of fuss,
just for two people, but then how could we have
done that if we had people coming and going all the
time like people have in London? It would have
been impossible. Just what the minister said,—
'When you are in Rome you must do as the Ro-
mans do.' I quite see what you meant about those
men that ran from the station to carry our luggage
in. We would always send anybody who came on
an errand to get a good meal in the kitchen, but how
could you do that in London with all the hundreds
and thousands that walk about the streets day and
night? Why, it wouldn't do. I am old enough
and I see that, and I do not mean to be a trouble
to you, Aunt Elinor. I am trying hard to get off
telling the truth so dreadfully because I see the
inconvenience of it, and I am sure, dear, you are so
kind and so patient with us, and I quite see what a
nuisance we must be to you. But the little ones,
you see they are young, and they do not understand
as I do that their first duty should be to please you,
or if not to please you,—because we must be a

dreadful trouble to you,—at all events, to be as little of a nuisance as they can. I am afraid that you will have a great deal of annoyance with us one way and another, and the only way for you to save yourself a little will be for you to be quite angry with the others and lay down some hard and fast rules that they must not transgress, such as interfering with the servants. I shall speak very severely to Honor about it by and by, because, after all, nothing is so important to us just now as to try to please you."

Miss Mortimer leant her head back against the slim shoulder of her tall young niece with a feeling of great affection and of extreme contentment. "Dear child," she said, with a suspicious tremble in her voice, "I think you will be a very great comfort to me during the next few years. It is no use my pretending to you, dearest, that for a woman of my fixed habits, living a solitary life as I have done for some years now, that it was not a matter of dread to me to even contemplate assuming the care of five young things of the age of yourself and your brothers and sisters. Of course, I want to make this the home of all of you. I want you to be as happy here in a different way as you were in your island up in the north; I want you to love me; you are the only relations that I have in the world, and I am your nearest, if not your only relation. I want us to be everything to each other. Of course, these little things are trying at first,—I won't pretend that they are not,—and nothing is so trying as what puts out old and valued servants. I am sure, darling, that you will do everything that is good and sweet; you will help me very much in this new responsibility of mine. You see, dear, you are used to your brothers and sisters, and to me it is all new. I feel sometimes that I am not old enough, nor grave enough, nor that I have had experience enough to be a suitable guardian to you. I was so many years younger than your dear father."

"Fifteen," said Ernestine, holding Miss Mortimer quite closely and looking down upon her with the protecting air which sixteen does sometimes assume to middle age. "Father has told me over and over again that you were fifteen years younger than he was, and he was sixty-five when he died."

Miss Mortimer's heart sank. She had hoped, not with any great degree of assurance, but still she had hoped that her brother Thomas had been merciful enough to leave the question of her age undiscussed with his young sons and daughters. Of course, it was too much to expect from Thomas. Miss Mortimer had never thought of herself as a woman of fifty. She had for some years past put her age at thirty-five; she had lived up to it, and she had dressed down to it; but if all these children knew that she was turned fifty, then it was good-bye to any hope of the whole world not sharing in the same knowledge.

"Dear Ernestine," she said, very gently, "I think, for your own sake, darling, I ought to tell you that in London it is not considered polite to discuss a lady's age. They say, you know, dear," with a little uneasy laugh, "that a man is as old as he looks, and a woman as old as she feels. Of course, I don't mind my age being talked about,"—which was a story, Miss Mortimer, if ever you told one in this world,—"but some people are very touchy upon this point. I would give the others a warning, dear, not to ask people their age or to talk about it; it would offend so many."

"Oh, I see," said Ernestine. "Is it that people are not thought so much of when they are old?"

"No, dear; but I don't know that any of us are better for being older. At all events, it is not——"

"Not quite the thing?" said Ernestine.

"No, not quite the thing. You will bear it in mind, won't you?"

"Oh, yes, auntie, I will bear it in mind. I will speak to the others most severely about it."

"Not severely, dear, because they have not in any way approached the subject."

"No, dear; but one cannot impress upon them too strongly when they are not to do certain things. If I had only known yesterday, or even this morning, that it is not polite to give a servant any information as Honor did just now, James would not have been upset, and you would not have been troubled with a visitor who was a nuisance to you."

"No, dear, not a nuisance, dear. I am afraid I cannot make you understand, but it is not my habit to receive except on certain days. Now do you understand?"

"Oh, yes, I understand perfectly. You would have been very glad to see this lady on your proper at-home day that you have on your visiting card, I understand exactly. But in future, dear, you tell *me* when there is any little thing that you want altered, because you see, I am used to the others, and I can make them understand where they might think you unkind, and I know you don't want that to happen."

"*Dear* Ernestine," murmured Miss Mortimer, in quite a gush of gratitude.

Ernestine's next remark fell upon her aunt's startled ears like the detonation of an explosion of dynamite. "Auntie," she said, "I never saw anything so curious as your hair in my life! It is red at the top, but it is quite black underneath!"

6

CHAPTER VI.

THE GRAVITY OF BEING THE ELDEST.

THE news of Miss Mortimer's changed circumstances very soon became known among her numerous acquaintances, and the first day on which she received after her brother's death and the arrival of his children in the house at Hans Place, the young people from Fynlan had an opportunity of learning what a numerous acquaintance really meant.

By that time Christmas had come and gone and the New Year was well advanced, it was, in fact, the second Tuesday in the first month of the year. Conveniently enough Miss Mortimer had not happened to send out cards after her return from her autumn journeyings, and on this, her first reception of the season, there was quite a flutter of excitement to see the new importations from the far north.

It happened that two of Miss Mortimer's most intimate friends met on the broad pavement in Hans Place, one having just got out of her carriage and the other having approached the door on foot. " How do you do, dear?" said the lady of the carriage. " You are going to Miss Mortimer's, of course ?"

"Yes, I am very anxious to see the new family."

"Ah, yes, I did hear something about it. Five young barbarians, I am told, who do the most awful things, and arrived fresh from their father's funeral a mass of tartan and eagles' feathers, and bare legs and so on."

"Oh, no, not really? But Elinor Mortimer will have altered all that."

"Well, I only tell you as I was told it. They say Elinor's hair has turned quite grey with the responsibility."

"Nonsense, my dear! Responsibility does not touch the hair of those who affect a henna-man! And between ourselves, since you and I have known Elinor Mortimer, she has had her hair every conceivable shade, from jet-black to a brilliant golden."

"I think the henna suits her best," said the lady, who had come in the carriage.

Then they turned towards the house together. Both ladies were favourites with the faithful James, who greeted them with the subdued, bland smile of an old acquaintance who was quite sure of his footing.

"Ah, James," said the carriage lady, with affable graciousness, "I need hardly ask if Miss Mortimer is at home."

" No, my lady, said James, urbanely. " Miss Mortimer will be delighted to see you; she has not seen much of her friends this winter."

"Ah, no, and she has had a loss since we parted at the end of the season."

"A very great loss, my lady. Sir Thomas, Miss Mortimer's brother, died very unexpectedly. It was a great grief to my mistress."

" I am sure it was," exclaimed the two ladies in a sympathetic murmur.

The bright-faced Rosine was ready in the study to relieve them of any wraps that they wished not to carry into the drawing-rooms. " There is one thing very pleasant about this house," said Lady Constance to Mrs. Valpé as they passed up the stairs together, "and that is that you find the same servants here year after year. James, of course, is an institution, and one would feel fearfully out of it if one were not an acquaintance of James'; but that bright-faced little French woman who takes your things and smooths you down, and generally makes you feel very much pleased with yourself, what a treasure she must be! My maid is such a fool."

" Mine is worse than a fool," said Mrs. Valpé; " more of the knave in her composition."

" Yes, I often envy Miss Mortimer her Rosine. It must be very delightful to have a Rosine and be able to keep her."

Then they passed into the smaller of the two drawing-rooms, and Miss Mortimer came forward to receive them. By this time she had very much light-
ened her mourning attire,—indeed, she was wearing
a tea-gown which gave but little of woe to her aspect.
It seemed to the two ladies that there was no necessity to mention their hostess's recent loss, so they
plunged at once into the latest town gossip. So far
they had seen no sign of the new importations, but
presently the door opened, and the slim, young figure
of Ernestine came quietly in. Certainly a few weeks
of association with her aunt, and life in a London
atmosphere, with the aid of a good London dress-
maker, had made a vast difference in Ernestine's appearance. She had struck Miss Mortimer as a lovely
young creature when she had arrived off a long winter journey, barbarously dressed in a hideous tartan.
Now, dressed as she was in suitable mourning attire,
not painfully deep in character, but of exquisite cut,
her sunny hair properly arranged by the skilful hands
of the artistic Rosine, she was as beautiful a young
creature as ever burst upon an expectant world.
Miss Mortimer looked up at her with much affection.
"This is my niece, Ernestine,—my eldest niece," she
said to Lady Constance.

"Ah, we heard that you had made great changes
in your household," said Lady Constance, sympa-
thetically. "How do you do, my dear?"

"Thank you, I am quite well," said Ernestine, in her ready and well-bred voice.

Then several other visitors were announced, and she was left to entertain her new acquaintances as best she could.

"And how do you like London?" asked Mrs. Valpé.

"Oh, we like it immensely—all of us. Of course, it is very different to our own home, because that was so large and so wild," said Ernestine; "but we are very fond of Aunt Elinor, and she is so kind to us."

"And your brothers and sisters, are they here too?" Lady Constance asked.

"Oh, yes, yes; they will be here in a minute or two." Ernestine looked towards the door with a certain degree of nervousness which was not lost upon the two ladies. "The truth is," said Ernestine, catching Lady Constance's eye, and with her wonderfully keen instinct realizing something of what was passing through her mind, "the truth is, I am a little anxious about them this afternoon. You see, I am the eldest, and I feel in a certain sense responsible for them—for them all. Children will get into mischief." She looked so sedate, in spite of her extremely youthful appearance, that neither lady was able to repress a smile. "Ah, you think I am very young," said Ernestine, "but then I have always been the eldest, and the others do not realize as I do what a nuisance we must be to Aunt Elinor. Now she has got her first party for this year, and I believe she expects a great many people, and naturally she does not want anybody to get into mischief to-day. Would you believe it, those four children are all down in the area at this moment dancing round an Italian hurdy-gurdy man with a wretched little monkey? They would not listen to me, and I was so angry that I came away. I sent Tammas down to them, but whether Tammas will be able to keep them from bringing hurdy-gurdy man and monkey up here is more than I am able to tell."

"My dear child," exclaimed Lady Constance, blankly, "one never knows what terrible diseases those hurdy-gurdy men may be carrying about with them! Has the man a baby?"

"No, a monkey," said Ernestine; "a wretched little creature with a cough which makes my heart ache," she added, fixing the older lady with her bright eyes.

"And who is Tammas?" asked Mrs. Valpé.

"Oh, Tammas is our piper. Tammas has great influence over the children,—very great influence. I—I—put him at the door, and I told him he was not to let the hurdy-gurdy man in, and I don't think he will. He said he could do better if I came away. Don't tell Aunt Elinor, because it will only worry her."

" And your piper, what does he do ?"

" Oh, he goes out with us if Aunt Elinor does not want to go. If the boys want to go anywhere, they are quite safe with Tammas, because you see, although he does not speak much English, he understands what they ought to do and what they ought not to do."

" And is he going to play for us this afternoon ?"

" Well, I suggested it to Aunt Elinor, but she seemed to think that London people would not care much about the pipes."

" Oh, I think they would. It would be something very new. I shall ask your aunt to let us hear Tammas," cried Lady Constance. " I know if I had a Tammas he should always play at my parties."

" Should he ?" Ernestine cried. " Well, I am sure if you would like to have him to your next party he will come with pleasure; only you must tell your butler not to give him too much whiskey or else, ten chances to one, he will get drunk. Not that he has been drunk—quite drunk, I mean—since we came from home, because I spoke to him most severely before we started, and again when Aunt Elinor decided that she would let him stop with us, and I told him if ever he got helplessly drunk he would just be put into the train and sent back to Fynlan, and, of course, Tammas being our body-servant our personal servant, I mean, he would feel that a great disgrace to be sent back like a bale of goods."

" I am sure he would.   Well, when I have a party I shall certainly ask Miss Mortimer if she won't lend Tammas to me."

"Oh, I am sure she will; she will be delighted. And Tammas will be so proud.   Oh, there they are! Clever Tammas!   He's got them up here without the hurdy-gurdy man or the monkey !"·

PART IV.

CHAPTER VII.

THE INCIDENT OF THE HURDY-GURDY MAN.

ERNESTINE MORTIMER had, however, reckoned without her host in imagining that her young brothers and sisters were going to behave in quite an ordinary way at this their aunt's first party. It is true that they all came into the room and were duly made known to the guests nearest to Miss Mortimer at the time. Their beauty, their charming, frank, and ingenuous manners had the effect of making quite a sensation among Miss Mortimer's guests. Then Georgie, who had been named after him who could not tell a lie, edged up to his aunt and preferred a request to her. "Aunt Elinor," he said, "you are going to let Tammas play the pipes this afternoon, aren't you?"

"Oh, I think not, my dear. They don't have that sort of thing in London," Miss Mortimer whispered back again.

"Oh, do!" he said; "Tammas will be so disappointed. He has dressed himself in all his best, and he is waiting in the hall now with his pipes under

his arm, just for you to give the word. Do auntie,
dear!"

A very smart lady who happened to be standing
near by overheard part of the request. "Do you
mean to say that your young nieces and nephews
have got their piper here?" she enquired.

"Yes," replied Miss Mortimer.

"And we want our aunt to let him play out in the
hall, you know," said Georgie, turning his brilliant
eyes upon the questioner.

"Oh, my dear, do. It will be such a novelty!
Ah, if I had a piper I would have him play—I should
think I would!"

"And Tammas plays splendidly!" cried Georgie.

"Very well," said Miss Mortimer; "tell Tammas
he may play, and I will tell him when to stop."

But Georgie hung back. "May Ernestine tell
him?" he asked, a little shyly.

"Yes, dear; but why can't you tell him?"

"Well, you see, Tammas is accustomed to taking
orders more from Ernestine than from us, and he
might think that you had not really given leave, do
you see, auntie?"

"Oh, very well." Miss Mortimer went across to
where Ernestine was still talking to Lady Constance.
"My dear," she said, "it seems that Tammas is very
anxious to play out in the hall, and two or three
people have asked if he might. Would you tell

him, dear? I will give him a hint when to
stop."

"Are you going to let him march through the
rooms, auntie?" Ernestine asked.

"Pray do!" said Lady Constance and Mrs. Valpé
in one breath.

"Well—just through the rooms, and then he may
play in the alcove—what do you think?"

The alcove was a wide landing with a deep bay
window, half window, half conservatory, that is to
say, it was a window which would shut off with doors
from the rest of the house, and was kept filled with
many beautiful green plants.

"Oh, I think that would be delightful," said Ernestine. "Tammas will be so proud. You can't think
how proud these pipers are, particularly if people
clap them, you know." And then she added in her
own mind, "I must run down and give James a
hint."

She found Tammas on guard in the lower hall,
dressed in all his best and awaiting a summons from
the mistress. Ernestine went up to him and told him
Miss Mortimer's wish, explained just how he should
walk through the drawing-rooms playing, and where
he should take up his station to wind up his per-
formance. James was also in the hall. Ernestine
went from Tammas to him and bade him in a whisper
to just take care that the Fynlan man did not get

tempted with too much whiskey afterwards. "You
will be obliged to give him a little whiskey, you
know, James, because you know it is the custom in
Fynlan, but don't give him too much."

"Very good, Miss Ernestine," said James, "I
quite understand."

Three minutes afterwards the crowd—it had really
become quite a crowd—in the drawing-rooms was
startled by the entrance of a stalwart person in Highland costume, who flung open the double-doors, and
marched in madly skirling an ear-splitting and
hideous tune from the bagpipes under his arm.
The young Mortimers danced on in front, filled with
glee, with the exception of young Sir Thomas, who
promptly disappeared from the scene.

Alas for Ernestine's anxieties! Alas for Miss
Mortimer's tardily given consent! Tammas, taken
off guard, had given his young master the opportunity to slip down and introduce the Italian hurdy-
gurdy man and his wretched little monkey into the
house, to smuggle them up the back staircase, and
to usher them into the drawing-room in the wake of
the proud and triumphant Tammas. As Tammas
passed out of the lesser drawing-room into the
larger one, the Italian hurdy-gurdy man was introduced therein.

For a minute or two the discordant tones of the
bagpipes completely drowned the lesser hideousness

of the hurdy-gurdy; then Miss Mortimer became
aware of a new interest among her guests. "What
is that?" she asked, turning her startled eyes upon
the folding-doors by which the two rooms commu-
nicated.

"It is an echo," said Georgie, who had been called
after Washington, "an echo."

A shout of laughter from the other room caused
her to turn her steps that way. Then there was a
violent shriek, followed by several ear-piercing yells,
which were not shouts of amusement by any means
—"Oh! oh! oh! Take it off! Take it off! What
is it? What is it? It is killing me! Oh! murder!
murder! murder!" was the agonized cry of a lady
dressed in the richest velvet and furs.

Miss Mortimer's horrified eyes fell upon the august form of her most distinguished guest, upon
whose ample shoulders the wretched little monkey
had sprung and perched himself like a veritable old
man of the sea. Before his master could order him
back to his own shoulders, this creature had possessed itself of a sable tail, a glittering ornament
from the lady's head-gear, and with the other monkey
hand had torn from her head something—something lightish-brown in tint and curly in nature,
which had nothing to do with her bonnet.

The hurdy-gurdy man spoke to it in guttural
Italian; you know the kind of Italian I mean, not

those liquid and enchanting sounds which we English people are accustomed to associate in our minds with the language of the sunny South, but that curious guttural cluttering which is perhaps a patois, or due to a want of education.

The actual scene was over in a moment, although the tragedy remained in *statu quo*, for in a trice the dark-visaged Italian person had transferred the gibbering monkey from the lady's shoulders to his own, and continued to address it in grave words of condemnation. The man was, however, in total ignorance that the monkey had retained its grip upon the sable tail, the glittering ornament, and the sunny, shining curls which had graced the top of the lady's head. These, to the exquisite enjoyment of everybody excepting Miss Mortimer and their owner, the small brown creature waved aloft in its skinny, hairy hands.

"Where did he come from?" cried Miss Mortimer. "Who brought him in here? Oh, dear, dear! Ernestine, Ernestine! Fetch James, my dear, fetch James and Tammas, and let them put this creature out of the room! Oh, my dear Lady Camdentown, I am afraid that dreadful beast hurt you. Pray come into my room and recover yourself a little."

Lady Camdentown meanwhile had sunk upon the nearest seat and had buried her burning face in her pocket-handkerchief. As James and the stalwart

Tammas came into the room, and with merciless
grip seized the hurdy-gurdy man and monkey, and
thrust them swiftly out, Miss Mortimer made an
equally valiant attempt to hustle the outraged and
injured lady into the seclusion and privacy of her
own boudoir, which was on the same floor as the
drawing-rooms. Lady Camdentown was, however,
too overcome by anger and hysterics to yield herself
to the ministrations of any one, and it was not until
two gentlemen had come to their hostess's aid that
she was induced to leave the room where she had
been, as she said, outrageously assaulted and in-
sulted.

The watchful James had, with singular prudence
and forethought, rescued the sable tail, the glittering
ornament, and the scalp of brown curls from the
greedy grasp of the little creature which had given
such delight to the young Mortimers. He brought
them presently to the door of the boudoir, at which
he knocked discreetly. The anxious face of his mistress appeared in answer to the summons. "I—I
rescued these things, ma'am," he said, with a discreet
cough. "I thought you would be sure to be putting the lady to rights before she went back into the
drawing-rooms. Shall I send Rosine to you, ma'am.
And would her ladyship like a glass of anything—a
glass of wine?"

"A little brandy and soda; make it rather strong,

James," whispered Miss Mortimer. "And send Rosine at once."

Lady Camdentown was lying in a deep chair with a large bottle of lavender salts, from which the stopper had been removed, at her elbow. "My dear Lady Camdentown," said Miss Mortimer, going back and carefully concealing the scalp behind her, "I have sent for a little restorative, and my maid will be here in a moment. They have rescued the ornament from your bonnet. I suppose it was a temptation to the little creature, they are so fond of gew-gaws."

"I shall never get over it," said Lady Camdentown, with a faint moan; "the awful shock—the dreadful, hairy feeling—the fearful blows it gave me on my head. Oh, dear, I shall never get over it!"

"No, dear, take a sniff of this, and James will bring a little restorative in two minutes. Rosine will soon put you right again. I can't think how the creature got into the house."

She tucked the scalp away out of sight behind some cushions, and began to gently undo the pins which secured Lady Camdentown's toque upon her dishevelled head. "No, stay quite still, dear. Don't move until James has brought you a little something to pick you up again. You do take a brandy and soda on emergency, don't you?"

"I will take anything—anything which will relieve this dreadful faintness," said Lady Camdentown, who,

like all other large and portly persons, was easily
ruffled and upset.

A gentle knock at the door warned Miss Mortimer
that the faithful James had returned with what she
was pleased to call a restorative. She went to the
door and took the little tray from his hands, knowing that her unfortunate visitor would not like to be
seen in her present dishevelled condition. Then
Rosine came and began with deft and gentle fingers
to reconstruct her ladyship. She replaced the ornament torn from the smart little toque, and rearranged
the sunny curls which had graced the lady's brow.
" My lady," she said, " if I were you I would just
add a *soupçon* of *rouge*—a little colour. It will prevent people saying too much of pity. I am afraid,
madam," she went on, turning to her mistress, " that
it was the naughty young ladies and gentlemen.
Miss Ernestine was most anxious that Tammas, the
great piper-man, should stay at the door below to
stop the musician with the monkey from making an
entrance, but when you ordered him to come and
play for the company, the door was left unguarded
and in zey came. Poor Mademoiselle Ernestine is
almost weeping. She is so ver' annoyed."

" Go and fetch her here, Rosine. I can't let her
think that I blame her. I am sure Lady Camdentown would not do so. She is so sweet, and good,
and dear, and the young brothers and sisters are

such a trial to her! Really, I don't know how I can sufficiently apologize to you for them."

Miss Mortimer wrung her hands together so piteously, and looked at her august visitor with such distressed eyes, that Lady Camdentown, serene in the feeling that she looked no worse for the adventure, and much comforted by the little restorative, smiled benignly, and was inclined to make very light of the whole thing. " Oh, well, dear, children will be children; you mustn't be angry with them. I daresay you and I did dreadful things when we were young. I know I did. But you confess it was rather startling to suddenly find oneself throttled by a pair of hairy arms and banged over the head at an ordinary innocent afternoon party, too. Don't let that pretty young thing feel that I blame her for it."

" Go and fetch Mademoiselle Ernestine," said Miss Mortimer to the maid. " She is such a dear child," she added, " it will be so kind of you to speak to her and keep her from feeling that she was to blame."

In truth, Miss Mortimer was not a little pleased that her pretty young niece should have attracted the notice of so great a social leader as Lady Camdentown. One of her pet theories was that it is impossible for young girls just entering upon society life to do without the countenance and interest of the acknowledged leaders of fashion. She felt that her

nieces were pretty, that they would have excellent
dots, and that the marriages of the two younger ones
would depend in a great measure upon the marriage
which was made by their elder sister; and, being
anxious to do her duty to them to the very utmost,
she was delighted in her heart of hearts to think that
Ernestine had attracted Lady Camdentown's attention.

Ernestine came softly in, full of anxious commis-
eration. "Oh, those naughty children!" she cried.
"And I was most particular in telling Tammas not
to let that man in. I had an idea they might do
something of the kind. Whatever did Lady Camdentown say? Were you much hurt? It was
dreadful for you. Aunt Elinor, you will have to be
most severely angry with them. I have told them
that the moment—if Lady Camdentown comes in
again—that the moment she comes in they will have
to make the most abject apologies to her. Really,
your friends will think that your nieces and nephews
are utter barbarians. I wish I hadn't left them at
all. They would not come in from the area, Aunt
Elinor, and I put Tammas on guard at the door, and
told him on no account was he to leave the spot
until the hurdy-gurdy man was actually gone. I
thought, when they all came into the drawing-room
looking so mealy-mouthed and so meek and so good,
that the danger was over, but one can never be really

four-square with those children. I know what
the end of it all will be—you will send us all to
school."

" No, my dear, no. Lady Camdentown is not very
angry."

" She was *very* angry," said Lady Camdentown,
with a jolly laugh, " but she is not angry now, dear.
You know children will be children, and we must
forgive them."

It was with this benign sentiment upon her lips
that Lady Camdentown signified to her hostess that
she was now ready to return to the general assembly.
" Really," she said, to the first friend she met on re-
entering the drawing-room, " I thought I was being
murdered. I never was so frightened in my life.
And poor Miss Mortimer is so annoyed. I am quite
sorry for her."

At this moment the four younger of the truth-
tellers, headed by the young Sir Thomas, approached
the august lady. " We have come to apologise abjectly to you," said Sir Thomas, looking her frankly
and fearlessly in the face; " we—we were very
naughty. We thought auntie's guests would like to
have the hurdy-gurdy man and the monkey because
we liked it ourselves. And, of course, we had no
idea the monkey would take liberties like those!
We apologize abjectly, all four of us."

" All four of us," murmured the others.

f

"Very well, very well—quite an accident," said Lady Camdentown, who was by this time quite as anxious to forget the occurrence as Miss Mortimer herself.

Georgie, who had been named after him who could not tell a lie, found his voice at this moment. " Yes, we apologize most abjectly," he said, pressing to his brother's side, " abjectly. And, of course, Lady Camdentown, we had no idea that the monkey was so badly behaved, and probably the monkey had no idea that your scalp would come off!"

CHAPTER VIII.

TOO MUCH OF A GOOD THING.

WITH many inward groans and misgivings Miss Mortimer had come to the conclusion that one may have too much even of a good thing. From her youth up she had been trained to regard truth as the most beautiful and blessed of qualities. We are most of us trained in the same belief and feeling, some of us perhaps prefer to give charity the premier place, but there are few of us in a civilized state of life who do not unhesitatingly give truth as the most beautiful of characteristics. We say a *true* gem, a *true* woman, such a *true* friend. If we ask the character of a servant, we almost invariably ask if they are truthful, and to say that a young child has a truthful disposition is at once to bias all our hearers in that child's favour. We have the *true* skin, a *true* poet, and we have remembered Alfred the Great during the hundreds of years that have passed since he lived and flourished, not so much because he was great, but because he was called the truth-teller.

Miss Mortimer had been brought up with a distinct appreciation of this beautiful virtue, but in the education of her nieces and nephews it had been brought to such a pitch of—shall we say *imperfection*, that she very soon learned to regard it as a most unpleasant, inconvenient, and detestable quality. The hardest part of it was that the young Mortimers were quite innocent themselves of giving any cause of offence by saying exactly what happened to come into their exceedingly open and ingenuous minds, all excepting Ernestine, that is to say, who was already sufficiently imbued with worldliness to see the wisdom of her aunt's desire to curtail in some degree the excessive frankness of her brothers' and sisters' comments on things in general and on personal matters in particular.

In due time the two boys went to a preparatory school for Eton, and then the prime originators of mischief being removed, life at the house in Hans Place became distinctly more tranquil in character. So far as Honor and Crystal were concerned, however, Miss Mortimer never felt sure from one moment to another that their too truthful tongues would not lead them to make some terrible and awkward disclosures.

I have said before that these children had been under the care of French and German governesses, and Miss Mortimer secured a first-class finishing Parisian governess, and dispensed with the services of the lady who hailed from the Fatherland. In the first place she had not room in her house for more than one stranger, and she was not inclined to give up her home in order to accommodate a second governess, besides, she had a great opinion of young girls being given the advantage of masters of distinction, and had no idea of her young nieces being coached up for solid study and examinations as if they were to become governesses instead of being fitted for ordinary society. Ernestine was already in her seventeenth year, and Honor less than two years younger, Sir Thomas was twelve, and Georgie ten and a half, while Crystal, the baby, was exactly a year his junior.

It would have been, of course, quite impossible for Miss Mortimer to take three young girls out and about with her, and while at first she had intended to take them turn and turn about, her dread of what they might say soon led to her only including Ernestine in any of her personal arrangements.

"I think, dear," she said one day to Honor, when that young lady was particularly anxious to go to a certain afternoon party with her aunt, "I think, dear, that I would rather take Ernestine. You see, she is older; she is almost a come-out young lady, and it will be your turn by and by, darling."

She flattered herself, poor lady, that she had quite satisfied her niece as to her reasons for making a preference in favour of the elder of the three girls, but a few days afterwards she realized with a shock that the workings of her mind were laid as bare to these young people as if they had that curious part of her being in tangible form under the lenses of a strong microscope.

Like many other very fashionable people, Miss Mortimer was most particular in attending to her devotions. She had not the smallest objection to remaining out during the small hours which follow Saturday evening, to attending receptions on Sunday, or, indeed, any festivity, but Sunday morning invariably found her in her place in a certain fashionable West End church. She was most particular in subscribing to various funds connected therewith, although she paid for her seat, and she duly and truly entertained the incumbent thereof, and such of the assistant priests as commended themselves to her fancy, at her hospitable table.

It happened one morning, two or three days after her little explanation to Honor about Ernestine being almost a grown-up young lady, that her especial spiritual adviser, otherwise the incumbent of St. Aloysius, came shortly before lunch time to consult her on some point connected with his church. " You will stay and have lunch with us ?" she asked. The reverend gentleman was in the habit of staying to lunch or to any other meal that came handy with his

fair parishioners, and accepted her invitation without
a moment's hesitation.

"Then you will not fail to give us a hand with
this sale of work, Miss Mortimer?" he remarked,
during the course of the meal, his thoughts reverting
to the errand which had brought him to the house.

"I should be delighted to do so, provided that I
could have the pottery stall," said Miss Mortimer.
"You know, vicar, that I have really no time to
gather needlework together. I don't mind giving a
stall if I can go to a big china shop and bid them
furnish it."

"You shall have what stall you like. I will make
that a fixture now."

"Do you think your committee will like it?" she
asked.

"Oh, my committee must like it," he said, quietly.
"If you wish to have the pottery stall, that settles
the question. And your charming nieces,"—with a
comprehensive look towards the dainty beauty of
Ernestine, who was seated at the foot of the table,
and the radiant countenances of the younger girls.
"I hope they will come and help. We want young
ladies. One cannot have too many young ladies,
you know, Miss Mortimer."

"Well, Ernestine will be delighted to come," said
Miss Mortimer, rather hurriedly.

"And not the others?"

"Well, Ernestine, for certain," Miss Mortimer said, graciously.

The clergyman looked puzzled. Honor explained the situation. "Aunt Elinor doesn't take us about very much, Mr. Vicar," she said, in her clear and ringing tones; "she did when we first came, but she doesn't now. She is always afraid we shall tell the truth."

"That you will do *what?*" he asked.

"She is always afraid that we shall tell the truth, aren't you, auntie?"

"My dear!" said Miss Mortimer.

"Well, you may say my dear, auntie, but that is it."

"Tell the truth?" repeated the vicar.

"Yes, we tell the truth. We were brought up to it," said Honor; "weren't we, Crystal?"

"Be quiet!" said Ernestine.

"No, I won't be quiet, Ernestine," said Honor. "It is the truth, isn't it, Crystal?"

"I believe we tell the truth too much," said Crystal, carefully avoiding her sister's warning eye.

"But you *can't* tell the truth too much," said the vicar; "that is quite impossible."

"Oh, yes, we do. We don't mean to, you know," Honor went on, "because, as auntie says, it is so dreadfully inconvenient,—most people don't like it,— but poor father would have it; and you have no idea, Mr. Vicar, how difficult it is to get into the way of telling lies!"

"My dear!" cried Miss Mortimer.

"Well, auntie, it *is* telling lies," Honor persisted. "Everybody in London tells lies. Only yesterday a lady came here, and I heard her say to her daughter as she went up-stairs, 'What a bore to find her in! I thought she would be sure to be out, a fine afternoon like this;' and when auntie went into the drawing-room I heard her say, "Dear Miss Mortimer, I am so delighted to find you at home! Now, what do you call that but lies?" she enquired, fixing her clear gaze upon the clergyman.

"Well—one couldn't call that exactly a lie," said the clergyman, with a laugh; "one would smooth that over and say it was—a little deception."

"That," said Honor, "is what our father would have called sophistry. I don't know what sophistry means, but whenever our minister at Fynlan tried to make father see that a thing wasn't a lie when it was, father always said, 'Duncan, that's sophistry!'"

CHAPTER IX.

THE BREAKING OUT OF TAMMAS.

ERNESTINE MORTIMER was an April child, and therefore attained the dignified age of seventeen years during the April immediately following her father's death. In the natural course of events Miss Mortimer would have advocated her remaining in the chrysalis stage until nearly another year had gone by,—that is to say, she would have introduced her formally into society with the beginning of the following year's season, but, after grave cogitation and serious consultation with one or two of her most trusted and valued friends, she came to the conclusion that her wisest plan would be to introduce her niece immediately after her seventeenth birthday.

" You see," she said to Lady Camdentown, who had remained a staunch friend and admirer of the elder of the three girls from Fynlan, " it is quite impossible for me to make any turn and turn about arrangement between Ernestine and the others. I can't even take Honor, who is old enough to be sensible,—just fourteen,—about with me very much. Poor dear children, they are very sweet and frank and open, and I am sure nobody values the beautiful

qualities of truth more than I do; but in their up-
bringing the love of truth has been carried to a passion—to an excess. I would not like to say so to
everybody, of course, and I can say things to you
that I really would not allow myself to say to anybody else in the world; but there are times when I
feel that if I could find one of my brother's children
out in a fib I should certainly give that one a sovereign as a kind of reward! It is a dreadful thing to
have said, my dear,—don't whisper it,—but such is
the weakness and wickedness of human nature that
I think I should positively welcome a sign of dis-
honesty."

"I don't know," said Lady Camdentown. "Of
course, to be bluntly outspoken is very inconvenient,"
and inadvertently her thoughts went back to the
open proclamation of her scalp, which the unconscious Georgie had shot at her devoted head not so
long before, "but you are spared any feeling of
sneakiness or deceitfulness. Now, I have a niece—
you know her, Mary Annandale—her mother was
my eldest sister, you know positively she cannot tell
the truth upon any subject whatever. Of course, her
friends know it, we all know it, and more than once
I have taxed her with it. I have said, 'You know,
Mary, that it is absolutely untrue; that never happened.' She has looked at me with her serene, blue
eyes, and has said, 'Yes, I know that it isn't true.

You are quite right, Aunt Cecilia, I do tell lies. I don't know why I do, but they come out somehow.' Now, you know, my dear," Lady Camdentown went on, "that sort of thing may be very amusing in a story-book, but it isn't very amusing in every-day life. Mary Annandale, for instance, is so fascinating, such a favourite in society, her husband and children are so nice, and everybody likes her so much that she naturally has a great deal of influence, and, even after all these years of knowledge of her, it comes upon me with a fresh shock each time that I realize that her word is not to be taken upon any subject."

"I have heard that about Lady Mary before."

"Oh, yes; it is quite an acknowledged thing in the family—quite. Oh, I think you may very much congratulate yourself on your five charges. They will grow older by and by, and they will see the inadvisability of giving expression to every thought which comes into their minds. Of course, Ernestine is quite charming, charming. You have no trouble with her."

"No. Ernestine sees very wisely. She is very frank and quite fearless, quite as ingenuous as her manner, but she has more sense than the others."

"Only because she is older, my dear," said Lady Camdentown, sapiently. "A couple of years of London will do wonders for those young people. I should not worry about it, if I were you."

" But would you bring Ernestine out now ?"

" Yes, I think I should. You see she is so pretty and so elegant, and she goes about so much with you that she has all the credit of being out and none of the advantages. If she were my niece I should certainly bring her out, and have her presented at one of the May drawing-rooms—by the bye, can I perform that little office for you ?"

"Oh, I should be so grateful," said Miss Mortimer. " It would be a real kindness. You see, poor child, having no mother and an unmarried guardian, she is dependent upon somebody outside her own family. It would be really very kind of you."

"I would do it with pleasure. I think I shall go to the second Drawing-Room. But we can arrange that later on. I think you would be much wiser to introduce her formally at once, because—or—it would be better for the other girls. I don't know that the second one won't be prettier than Ernestine."

"Oh, no !" said Miss Mortimer. Ernestine was her favourite.

" Well, I don't know. She is at an awkward age. She is exceptionally pretty, sweetly pretty, and she has a great deal of character, a wonderful amount of character for a girl of fourteen."

" I wish she had rather less," said Miss Mortimer, drily.

So in due course, Ernestine was introduced to the gay world, and presented to her sovereign. She made a delightful *débutante*, and was quite a sensation in her small way. She wore only white that season, being still in mourning for her father, and she was remarked chiefly for some wonderful pearls which had come down to her from her mother.

Miss Mortimer would hardly have believed six months before that she could have been so happy in the continual care of a young girl. So far from being in any way a burden on her aunt, or of making her seem older, she had the effect of making her feel and look much younger. Then, too, Ernestine being a fully-fledged society damsel, relieved her aunt of any necessity for making explanations to Honor as to the desirability of Ernestine being her constant companion. Ernestine was out, Honor was still in the school-room ; the question was settled definitely once for all. There could be no idea now of a come-out young lady giving place to one still in short frocks in the school-room. So the younger girls' jaunts with their aunt consisted almost entirely in driving with her occasionally of an afternoon, when they sat with their backs to the horses, and had not the smallest chance of getting into any kind of mischief. On such occasions, Miss Mortimer always made the drive into a little festivity by stopping to give them ices somewhere, or taking them to one of the American sweet-shops, so plentifully scattered about the metropolis.

On the whole, life went very much more smoothly at the house in Hans Place than it had done in the early days of the new state of affairs. The boys were doing well at their school, and the younger girls, although they were not shut up or in any way snubbed, did not quite take life in common with their elders, as they had been accustomed to do at Fynlan, which, as Miss Mortimer could not help seeing, was very much better for them.

There were, however, drawbacks to the influx of the family from Fynlan Castle which sufficed to keep Miss Mortimer in a state of continual uneasiness. She did not find the presence of Tammas, the piper, at all an unmixed blessing, and yet she was not sufficiently strong-minded to say boldly at once that she would prefer his room rather than his company. For one thing she felt that there was nothing for him to do, that he had no proper position in the house. She had tried, with the help of the faithful James, to make him what is called a handy man, but, on the whole, it cannot be said that this experiment turned out anything but a failure. Tammas was a piper, and Tammas took care that he was made nothing else. Under the severe eye of Miss Ernestine, he managed to keep tolerably straight in the matter of his takings, for some time after the arrival of the young people

in Hans Place. On one or two occasions Ernestine
had carpeted him very severely for signs which she
recognized as a probability of breaking out, but these
approaches to misdemeanour had been carefully concealed from the mistress of the house. But, alas,
even Ernestine's influence was not all lasting, and
one day the faithful James entered Miss Mortimer's
room with a very portentous expression upon his
solemn countenance.

" I am sorry to say, ma'am," said James, " that
Tammas has just returned home very much the
worse for liquor."

" Oh, dear, dear, dear!" cried Ernestine. " How,
where did Tammas get the money to get drunk with ?"

" My dear," said Miss Mortimer, promptly, " I paid
Tammas's wages only yesterday."

" Yes, auntie, I know it. But he sent home the
whole of the money you gave him to put in the
bank, as he usually does. I know it, because, you
know, he always gets me to write his letters to the
minister who manages his little affairs and pays his
mother her weekly allowance. His mother is very
old," Ernestine went on, " oh, so old that nobody in
Fynlan knows exactly how old she is. Tammas
always pays her rent—that isn't much—" she said,
parenthetically, " but he always sends her so much a
week, and he always likes to send the minister an
even sum, so this time, as he had had to buy some

things for himself, I lent him half-a-crown to make it the usual even money."

" You think that he really did spend the money ?"

" Oh, yes, auntie," said Ernestine. " Tammas would not tell a lie about a thing like that. Besides, he showed me the things that he had bought—pocket-handkerchiefs and things of that kind. You know Fynlan people are so simple, and he was so distressed about not having even money to send to the minister because he thought the minister would think he had been extravagant. And, after all, he didn't suggest borrowing of me; it was I who proposed lending to him."

As soon as Tammas was in a fit condition to be interviewed by the ladies of the household he was summoned to the small, plainly furnished room which Miss Mortimer dignified by the name of her study. It was a curious relic of olden days at the Chase which had prompted her to furnish a room which was naturally adapted for a gentleman's rather than a lady's use, in remembrance of a similar room which had been sacred to her father's concerns in the home of her ancestors. It was not an apart-ment which was much used. Miss Mortimer always interviewed servants there, whether it might be to give the orders to the coachman for the day, to interview the cook about the dinner, to engage new ones, or to reprimand such domestics as might hap-

pen to be in fault. She also saw any necessary
tradesman in the study, and on her reception days it
was always given up to the hats and coats of the
gentlemen who came to visit her. It was, in fact,
used strictly for business or for mere convenience.
Miss Mortimer's weekly account books were always
collected there, and she kept her cheque book in one
of the drawers of the large, severely plain, oak
writing-table. So little of a sitting-room was it that
it boasted of no fireplace, but was warmed at such
times of the year as warmth was necessary by an
asbestos gas fire which James always lighted in
readiness for his mistress' use as soon as he had
seen her fairly established at her breakfast.

It was in this room that the dread interview with
Tammas took place; Miss Mortimer was quite nervous about it. "Now, Ernestine," she said, when
the time drew near for the interview, "don't you
think, darling, that you had better be the spokes-
woman? You see, Tammas talks such broken
English, and it always seems to me that, when any
one has any little fault to find, he is more dense at
understanding than when he has something pleasant
to say. I suppose it is human nature," she went on,
"and that there is a good deal of truth in the old
saying that none are so deaf as those who won't
hear. Of course, you have the immense advantage
of being able to launch out into Gaelic."

Ernestine turned her brilliant eyes upon her aunt with an expression which Miss Mortimer had never seen in them before. "Aunt Elinor," she said, " I am most seriously angry with Tammas. I shall speak most *severely* to him. I warned him of his besetting sin when we first came from Fynlan, and I shall tell him to-day that this is his very last chance. Yes, I really do think, auntie, although you are mistress and Tammas knows it, that he will take more notice of me than he would do of you in this matter, because, as I shall tell him, you will be guided entirely by me and what I say. I will keep to English as long as I can ; and, if I do go off into a perfect blaze of Gaelic, you must not be frightened, dear, because I shall be very severe with Tammas indeed."

Her young niece's determination to show the recreant Tammas but small mercy had the effect of making poor Miss Mortimer even more nervous than she had been beforehand. She was a woman who loathed everything approaching to a scene. A quarrel was detestable to her, an uproar was quite sufficient to unstring her nerves for several days, and it was with a sinking heart and her whole nature positively palpitating with nervousness that she followed Ernestine into the dull little room where she transacted her affairs of business.

One minute later the stalwart figure of Tammas blocked up the doorway. Miss Mortimer looked up at him with apprehensive eagerness. She had expected to see a downcast, hang-dog-looking Tammas, thoroughly ashamed of himself, penitent, and, to a certain extent, suffering. Poor Miss Mortimer! In the simple giant from Fynlan there was no trace of shame, still less of suffering. He had been out to the stables, and he had got the coachman to play the carriage-hose over his head, which still glistened with the drops of water which lay among its crisp red curls. To look at him, a casual observer might have been forgiven for swearing that the man had never been drunk in his life, for there he stood, bold, upright, simple, and honest, a very picture of a man, his blue eyes as clear as a child's, his manners beautiful, unperturbed, quietly respectful, and sturdily inde-pendent. For a moment Miss Mortimer thought that the faithful James must have been mistaken. Not so Ernestine. She knew Tammas better than did the lady of the house.

"Tammas," she said, in stern, cold accents, "Miss Mortimer hears that you have been taking too much whiskey."

Tammas replied without a moment's hesitation that there must be some mistake; that he had had what he called a "wee drappie," but he certainly had not had too much; that he could safely have put away several more drinks than he had had the chance of having.

" But you came home drunk," said Ernestine.

" Na, na," Tammas replied, without the smallest hesitation; " she were no drunk at all; she had had a wee drappie; and she has been so long without a taste of the whuskey that her heid dinna carry it quite as weel as usual; but drunk, na, na, Miss Ernestine and mem, she were no drunk,—she had had just a wee drappie."

" Well, Tammas," said Miss Ernestine, standing up by the table and looking at the red-bearded giant with a cold, calm, and critical gaze, "you may choose to call it a wee drappie and you have got over it in fairly good time, so I daresay you were right in saying that you could have taken more, but, at the same time, here in London people call that getting drunk, and if the police had seen you, Tam-mas, they would have locked you up for a certainty."

" She kept out of the way of the poleece," re-marked Tammas, a sardonic grin hiding itself under his red beard. " There was one poleece what called her a 'Scotchie,' and she went by very quick so that she should keep her hands off her."

Miss Mortimer turned away to hide her laughter. but Ernestine was as grave as a judge.

" Well, Tammas, it may seem very funny to you," she said, " to go out of a respectable house in a town where people do not get drunk, or where, at all events, it is considered a great disgrace for men and

women to get drunk, but Miss Mortimer sees nothing
funny about it, and if I tell her you are to go back
to Fynlan in *disgrace* she will not hesitate to send
you back again.   I daresay Miss Mortimer will let
you off this once, as far as being drunk is concerned,
but she will not let you off a second time.   The
most important question, however, is where did you
get the money to get drunk with ?"

Now if a young lady had put such a question to
an ordinary English domestic, there would probably
have been the kind of scene for which Miss Mortimer
had nervously prepared herself.   The simple and
ingenuous mind of Tammas, however, saw no offence
in it.

"You know, Tammas," Miss Ernestine went on,
still standing up very straight beside the table, "it
was only yesterday that I lent you half-a-crown so
that you might make the money for the minister
even.   Now, if you had money to go out and get
drunk on, you need not have borrowed that half-
crown from me."

Still, Tammas looked perfectly unabashed.   "For
herself, Miss Ernestine," he replied, unhesitatingly,
"she had not so much as a bawbee in her pocket.
She went out yesterday and she met with Angus
Macdonald——"

"Angus Macdonald?" exclaimed Ernestine. "What,
from Fynlan?"

"The same, mem," said the unabashed Tammas.

"And what is Angus Macdonald doing in London, pray?"

"Well, mem," said Tammas, "Angus has lang been tired of Fynlan, and the winter was haird and the season was bad, and Augus, she got restless, and she came ower to the mainland, and there she enlisted."

"What!" cried Ernestine, in a sharp, staccato tone.

"Ou aye," replied Tammas, speaking in a tone of perfect equality—not equality of station, mind you, *that* never happened—but in perfect human equality, with no trace of shame at his late escapade lingering about him. "And she is now dressed up in a smart scairlet uniform, and she ca's herself ane of the Royal Horse Guards. She went out yesterday and she met wi' Angus, and Angus said to her, 'Tammas, will she gae and hae a wee drappie?' and she said, 'Ou aye,' and she had been sae lang wanting a wee drappie that her heid gav' oot."

"Well, Tammas," said Miss Ernestine, very severely, "I am glad that you were able to give my aunt an explanation of how you came to get into that disgraceful state—and, of course, it accounts for it—and I think she is satisfied this time, but you had better bear in mind, Tammas, that in future when you meet Angus Macdonald you had best leave wee

drappies out of the bargain. Probably Angus is
now in the cells and undergoing some dreadful pun-
ishment, such as you ought to have given to you.
However, as you have explained yourself, I shall
ask Miss Mortimer to let you off for this once; but
the next time you come in in a state to disgrace my
aunt's house and bring shame and discredit upon
ourselves, I shall ask for no explanation from you;
you will have your orders to go back to Fynlan at
once,—and to stop there!"

"She will remember," was Tammas's unexpected
reply. And then he bade the two ladies good-morn-
ing and betook himself out of their presence as unabashed and as sturdy as if such a thing as a wee
drappie of whiskey had never entered into his calcu-
lations.

When the door was safely closed behind him,
Ernestine and Miss Mortimer looked at one another
and went off into perfect convulsions of mirth.

"I knew he would be able to explain himself," said
Ernestine. "They are so simple, these Fynlan people; they are foolish and they get drunk; but they
do not tell lies, and they are quite honest."

"You knew who this Angus Macdonald was,
Ernestine?"

"Oh, yes, dear. He is one of the young men in
the blacksmith's shop,—really an armourer. His
father is our head game-keeper. I think there are

eighteen or nineteen of the young Macdonalds, and
Angus was the third boy,—yes, the third boy. They
are very fine fellows, all of them. I don't wonder he
got tired of Fynlan, for there is no enterprise there,
no getting on, no seeing anything, no learning anything; the other two boys ran away, and I don't
wonder at it. He will make a splendid soldier, and,
being such a first-class workman, he will probably
get on very well indeed in his new life."

"I think," said Miss Mortimer, "that Tammas
might have had the grace to be a little more ashamed
of himself."

"My dear auntie," said Ernestine, "the men in
Fynlan get drunk as a matter of course whenever
they have the chance. My wonder is that Tammas
has kept off it as long as he has done. He is very
devoted to us; I think that is the real reason. In
an ordinary household he certainly would have been
drunk within a week of his coming here; and you
know, dear, this is the first time, and he could not
have been very bad."

"No. But still, Ernestine, it is not the kind of
thing to pass over, particularly with a household like
ours, which has no master," said Miss Mortimer, a
little nervously. "I can only hope that your warning will have a good effect upon him."

"Oh, yes, dear; he won't break out again for a
long time," said Ernestine, confidently.

CHAPTER X.

Miss Mortimer's ideas for spending the summer holidays were to go for a visit to the Chase, which the children had never seen. Ernestine had been there, but had no recollection of it. "If we go for a month or so," said Miss Mortimer to Ernestine, "we could go straight up to Fynlan from there if you should still all be very anxious to do so. I think it is high time that Thomas should see his inheritance and the home of his ancestors. The Chase is a lovely spot, which to me is full of tender memories. It will be a great pleasure to me to take you young people there for the first time, and then you shall take me either now or one day to see your island home. I think if we go down to the Chase next week, that by that time I shall have got all the boys' things ready for them. I must have them for a week in town to do that, and I feel," Miss Mortimer went on, "that I shall be quite glad to get away into the fresh pure country air."

As a matter of fact, Miss Mortimer had but little intention of going to Fynlan that autumn, and she meant to make the Chase so pleasant to her charges

106

that they would themselves wish to remain there in preference to making the long journey to the far north.

When Miss Mortimer conveyed her final decision as to her autumnal plans to the ears of the faithful James, she gave him at the same time the information that she would go over the plate with him on the Wednesday in order that he might convoy all the valuables which the house contained to the strong-room of her bank, as was their regular habit and custom. The faithful James's face beamed with satisfaction. He, poor soul, had been dreading for some months past that his duty would require him to accompany his mistress and the young ladies and gentlemen to that terrible castle of theirs, that fastness away up in the north which could not be reached without a loathly five hours' journey over the briny ocean; so the news that they were going to the Chase was sufficient to make him extremely well pleased with his lot. James had no love of a life on the ocean wave. His idea of enjoying the sea was to spend a fortnight in Margate when his mistress was safely taking a cure at Homburg or Schwalbach. Then the faithful James might have been seen by such as knew him, arrayed in a suit of light check dittoes, with a straw hat upon his respectable head, sunning himself along the arid front, or in more select fashion enjoying the delights of the

health-giving breezes at the extreme end of the pier,
—the part where you pay twopence. The faithful
James did not disdain a trip to Boulogne by one of
the handsomely-appointed vessels which frequently
called at Margate for the purpose of dropping pas-
sengers from London and taking others on to the
French watering-place; but to spend five mortal
hours, at the least, in an evil-smelling steamer, reek-
ing of fish and oil, among gibberish-speaking persons
after the pattern of Tammas, was quite another
matter; and although James was too faithful and too
entirely devoted to his mistress's interests to dream
of trying to shirk the responsibility which accrued
to the position of her henchman, he yet hailed the
forthcoming visit to the Chase with unmixed feelings
of delight and satisfaction.

At last the arrangements for the mighty move
were made, and they all found themselves in the
beautiful old home which for hundreds of years had
been the cradle of the Mortimer race. It would be
hard to say how keen was the delight of the young
Mortimers at finding themselves once more enjoying
the pleasures of a country life. Each and all were
equally enthusiastic over the beauties of what was
really their ancestral home, though it was all very
different to what it would have been had the family
lived at the Chase as they had done at Fynlan. The
gardens were well-kept, but were not such gardens

as you find under the keen eye of a master; the game was poorly preserved; the stables were empty, except for Miss Mortimer's horses and for one or two animals which were needed by those who had care of the place. It was the same with the house. The rooms had that curious look of primness and almost of decay which rooms that have been long disused acquire. Everything was clean and bright, and there were many treasures, but the whole place lacked the hand of a mistress. It was most of anything, as Ernestine said to her aunt, like a body without a soul. And yet the young Mortimers each and all loved it; for one thing, there was plenty of room.

The neighbours came flocking to call, old friends whom Miss Mortimer had not seen for many years, and others who had made the neighbourhood their own since she had last been there. The young heir was petted and made much of, and, with his sisters and younger brother, were not only the observed of all observers, but by far the most popular young people to be found for miles and miles around.

"They are delicious!" said people to one another. "So frank, so fresh, so unconventional! Who would have thought that that silly Lady Muriel could have had such absolutely delightful children."

As Miss Mortimer felt more than doubtful whether they would be able to get as far afield from London as Fynlan during that autumn, she took much more pains to make herself and her young charges at home at the Chase than she would have done if they had been paying little more than a flying visit. In less than a week a radical change had come over the entire house, for Miss Mortimer made many judicious purchases with a view to present comfort and future use, and it was wonderful how soon the desolate look of the rooms began to wear away and the entire mansion to assume that air of comfort and elegance which is characteristic of most of our great country houses.

By the time that the incumbent of St. Aloysius (religiously called " Vicar " or " Father " by all his lady parishioners) arrived to pay his promised few days' visit, the Chase was looking as comfortable and as homelike as hostess or guest could wish to see. The chief anxiety at this time in Miss Mortimer's life was the fact that the neighbourhood persistently refused to allow the Mortimer family to be represented by herself and Ernestine, and she passed her days in continual terror of the awful revelations which might be made by the four younger children.

" It is quite impossible," she said to her clerical guest, " to make people understand the very peculiar bringing up that these children have had. Now, there is old Lady Hervey-Paget. Dear me, vicar, I remember her—oh, well, when I was a little girl—

and I remember thinking how extraordinary-looking she was then. She is much more extraordinary-looking now, and I think she rouges more and wears even more wonderful garments than she used to do then. I am so terrified that they may say something about her curls, or her cheeks, or her eyes, or something."

"But the old lady is very deaf, Miss Mortimer," said Mr. Delamere, easily, "she is very deaf."

"But she is not the only one!" exclaimed Miss Mortimer. "They are dear children, but they do keep me on tenter-hooks. Now, only yesterday, Mrs. Greville Sydney was here, and she asked them all to come over and spend a long day with her. I suggested that Ernestine and Thomas should go— Thomas is getting a sensible boy, school has done wonders for him, and Ernestine, of course, is a darling, I could trust her anywhere—but nothing would satisfy her except having all five of them for a long day. I said I would talk it over, at which Crystal laughed outright, and that tiresome little Honor made an elaborate explanation to Mrs. Sydney that I hesitated to let them accept because I was so afraid of their telling the truth. As I explained to her afterwards, it is not the truth I am afraid of, it is their general gaucheness. But there, I cannot make them understand. I suppose it will wear off in time, as it has done with Ernestine."

"Oh, yes, I would make my mind easy about it. After all if people don't like them, they needn't ask them again. Your friends have the remedy in their own hands," said Mr. Delamere, easily.

There is nothing so easy as to bear the woes and troubles of other people, and the easy way with which the Vicar of St. Aloysius dismissed his hostess's anxiety as to the future conduct of the young Mortimers did not tend in any way to give ease to that poor lady's perturbed mind. Under the care of a first-class governess, she had found her younger nieces, Honor and Crystal, wonderfully improved, and she had almost ventured to hope that her worst troubles had come to an end. When they went to the Chase, however, the amiable French lady, who had been chosen by Miss Mortimer to mould her young nieces into more conventional lines than had been theirs under their father's system, had departed for her native country on a seven weeks' holiday, and to her cost, when she found herself fairly settled at the Chase, Miss Mortimer discovered that there was still a great deal of the old Adam left in them. It may have been the fact that there was no smiling Parisian dragon to check them when they became too communicative; it may have been that the homecoming of the boys had had something infectious about it; anyway, certain is it that Miss Mortimer's fears proved not to be groundless, and she was soon

assured with certainty of the truth of the old
adage,—

"Satan finds some mischief still for idle hands to do."

Not that they were mischievous in the ordinary
sense in which we use the word; oh, dear, no.
They behaved quite beautifully; their manners, saving
for that intensely inconvenient habit of telling the
exact truth, the whole truth and nothing but the
truth, were delightful; even although two days after
the advent of the Vicar of St. Aloysius, little Honor
startled a large luncheon-party invited to meet him,
by saying in a sweet, shrill voice, " Vicar, did you
ever *really* know a maid-servant who got up an hour
earlier every morning that she might do the work of
another one who had a weak chest ?"

For a moment there was profound silence. The
entire conversation was suspended, and the majority of the guests waited in amused expectation
of what one of those "delicious" children was after
now. I say the majority, because there were three
persons at that table who looked as they felt, as if
they could have wished that the earth would open
and swallow them.

" Honor, dear," interrupted Miss Mortimer, " don't
talk so much."

" No, auntie," returned Honor, promptly; " but we
have got to the third course, and this is the first time
I have spoken."

h   10*

" Well, dear, well; but don't worry the vicar."

" She doesn't worry me, Miss Mortimer," said the vicar, assuming an ease which he was far from feeling. Then he turned to the child. " Little woman," he said, with a great assumption of friendliness, " you are thinking of the sermon I preached yesterday. As a rule, clergymen do not like to discuss their sermons in public. We will have a talk about it by ourselves presently, later on."

" I didn't want to discuss it, vicar," said Honor, quickly; " I was only wondering whether it was the same maid-servant that Mr. Jones knew."

Mr. Jones was the curate of the parish in which the Chase stood. As a matter of fact, the two gentlemen had preached the same sermon on consecutive Sundays, one of a convenient series written and published by a certain distinguished preacher, well known as a stand-by to many a parson less able in composition than himself, and the fact had puzzled Honor not a little, for she, truthful child that she was, had accepted a certain vivid and striking incident as the personal experience of both the gentlemen who had retailed it.

It would be hard to say whether the cheeks of the Reverend Bertram Delamere or those of the Reverend Edward Jones were the more reddened. Then the younger of the two looked at the fashionable London vicar, and had the good sense to burst out laughing. "A simultaneous bowl-out, sir," he said, with ingenuous ease.

"Jones, my dear fellow," said the vicar, an hour later, when they were walking on the terrace together; "I hope that one day you will get a bishopric."

It was in vain that Miss Mortimer afterwards, I mean after all her visitors had gone, took Honor most severely to task for the unfortunate question which she had asked that day. "My dearest child," she said, "how many times am I to tell you that it is not well-bred for little girls to ask questions?"

But Honor was not in the least abashed. "It seems to me, Aunt Elinor," she said, deliberately, "that it was not the question which was the difficulty, but the answer."

"My dear child, it was no business of yours."

"But, auntie," Honor exclaimed, "I have to go to church, and I have to listen to these sermons, and when I hear two clergymen preach the same sermon two Sundays together, it seems to me that I have got a right to ask a question about it."

"It doesn't matter whether they happened, by pure accident, to preach the same sermon or not, my dear child. A clergyman is not bound to preach his own sermons; some clergymen *cannot* write sermons. Our vicar, for instance, is far too busy to do so, and

Mr. Jones is probably much too young to have had
sufficient experience to write sermons. You must
not think that it is wrong, because it distinctly says,
'shall read a sermon or a homily.' There is no
obligation on any clergyman always to preach his
own sermons."

"Well, auntie," said Honor, staring at Miss Mortimer with wide open eyes, "all I can say is this,—
Mr. Jones said one Sunday that he knew a maid-
servant who got up one winter a whole hour earlier
that she might do the hard work of a fellow-servant
who had a delicate chest. That was what Mr. Jones
said,—' *I* once knew a servant.' Well, now, if it was
not his own sermon, and it wasn't the vicar's sermon,
how can either of them have known her? They
didn't; but they both told lies. And it seems to me,
auntie, that for a clergyman, who is supposed to know
better than we do, to get up in the pulpit and tell
lies is extremely wicked."

Miss Mortimer positively groaned. "I shall never
make you understand, you unfortunate children. It
is the dreadful way you have been brought up. I
am sure I never asked such questions when I was a
child. My dear Ernestine, I give you my word,
our clergyman at home, the old vicar I told you
about, might have preached the same sermon every
day for a year, and I should never have known
it."

"But you were not brought up to tell the truth, auntie," said Honor at that moment. She said it without the smallest attempt at sharpness, or without the least intention of being in any way impertinent; the thought came into her mind and her lips immediately gave utterance to it.

"Auntie was brought up very much more reasonably than we have been," said Ernestine, suddenly breaking into the conversation. "You are very little, and you do not yet understand how intensely stupid and annoying you are when you take this critical tone with everybody and everything."

"Father always said——" began Honor.

"Yes; but what father said at Fynlan does not apply to what Aunt Elinor says at the Chase," said Ernestine, promptly.

"It seems to me," said Honor, "that what vicar says when we go to church does not apply to anything that we do out of church."

"That is nonsense," said Ernestine.

"No, it is not nonsense, Ernestine," returned Honor, sturdily. Honor was great at sticking to her point. "Only two days before we left London, Crystal and I went to a children's service at St. Aloysius. Mademoiselle went with us. She said it was beautiful,—almost as good as the Oratory; and vicar himself stood on the steps by the altar railing, and he said, 'Children,'—and here Honor started

to her feet, raised her little chubby arm with a
gesture of exhortation,—' Children, remember now
and always that there is nothing so precious in this
world as *the truth*. *The truth* can never lead you
wrong. Speak *the truth*, the bare truth, and you
will be always right. You are young; most of
you have been born in a sphere where, I am sorry
to say it, one of the greatest every-day vices is the
habit of telling little lies,—white lies,—which are
thought to be of no account. But do you, my young
friends, stand up straight and true and resolute and
dare to tell *the truth*. It will serve you when all
fashionable fobbles——' "

"She means foibles," put in Ernestine.

"'——will have failed you,'" Honor went on.
"'If your mothers say "not at home" when they *are*
actually in the house, do not you take leave to yourself to tell little lies of the same kind. Remember,
in the sight of God there is no difference between
the little lie and the great lie; remember that there
is a *recordant* angel——' "

"She means recording angel," put in Ernestine.

"'——that there is a recordant angel who takes
note even of the lie which has no words, the lie which
is never told, the lie that is implied. I knew a child
once,'" Honor went on, with uplifted finger, and
preaching eloquently into a corner of the room, "'I
knew a child once, a little waif and stray, crippled,

distorted, racked with agony. That little child saw
a foul murder committed, and the man who committed the murder made that shrinking, terrified, helpless
little creature swear never to *diverge* what she had
seen——' "

" She means divulge," put in Ernestine.

" ' And when the police came, and questions were
put as to what that little girl-child had seen, she
spoke—*the truth.* " I saw the murder done," she
said. " I know who did it; but he made me swear
that I would never diverge it——" ' "

" Divulge," said Ernestine, in a low voice.

" ' " You may kill me, but I will keep my word." '
I thought it was all true," said Honor, in a different
tone; " but I believe now that it was as big a lie as
that maid-servant he told us about. I shall never
believe in Father Delamere again."

Miss Mortimer felt that her duty as a good church-
woman and as a friend of Mr. Delamere's was to try
at least to explain to this well-meaning but ill-regu-
lated child's mind that, even had Father Delamere
not known either the crippled child or the heroic
maid-servant, to use such incidents for the purpose
of dramatic illustration was not to constitute telling
a lie. She was a good woman and a good friend;
for a worldly woman she was exceedingly sincere.
But, alas, alas! sincerity got the better of her at that
moment, for she caught something like a twinkle in

Ernestine's blue eyes, and, I am sorry to say it, she went off into shrieks of laughter. So the chance of imparting an excellent lesson to Honor was entirely lost.

CHAPTER XI.

THE most terrible part of Miss Mortimer's position with regard to her young charges was that she utterly failed in bringing any of them, excepting Ernestine, to see the justice as well as the wisdom of her requirements. They were each and all genuinely fond of their aunt and guardian, and, although they were all equally ready to express the utmost contrition when any of their doings annoyed her or troubled her, yet she could never bring them to acknowledge that they had been in the wrong. More especially was this the case with Honor.

" Dear auntie," she said more than once, " I would not vex you for all the world."

" But you do vex me," said Miss Mortimer, one day, trying to be particularly stern. " It is really exceedingly naughty of you, Honor, to always do the things which I tell you you must not do. What could induce you this afternoon to tell Lady Hervey-Paget that her teeth rattled like castanets? It was most rude of you. I shall really have to forbid you the drawing-room, if you insult my friends in that way."

" I didn't tell her that her teeth rattled like castanets," said Honor, stoutly. "All I said was, that I understood now what people meant when they said that teeth rattled like castanets."

" But, child, where did you pick up such a phrase ?"

" I read it in a book," said Honor, sturdily. " I was reading a book the other day in the library about ghosts——"

" Oh, dear, dear !" ejaculated Miss Mortimer.

" Well, I am very sorry, auntie. I didn't know that I mightn't have it. You told me I could take any book I liked, and I took a book full of ghost stories. They are beautiful ! I am quite frightened to go to bed."

" And what about teeth rattling like castanets ?"

" Well, auntie, it describes a young lady who was so frightened at the ghost she saw that her teeth rattled in her head like castanets. I asked Ernestine what castanets were, and she told me they were those things that Spanish ladies rattle in their hands when they dance. I thought it was very queer that anybody's teeth should rattle like that, but when I saw Lady Hervey-Paget, I didn't think it was queer at all."

" But, my dear child, you should not have told her so."

"Auntie, I am very sorry; but I didn't say anything about *her* teeth."

"No, but you said, '*Now* I understand how teeth can rattle like castanets,' and, of course, she knew you meant her teeth. I expect she will never come here again."

"Well, auntie," said Honor, in a desparing tone, "I should not think you would mind very much. She is a dreadful old lady."

"My dear child!"

"Oh, yes, she is, auntie; she is very dreadful. And I am sure she doesn't like you."

"That is nonsense! Lady Hervey-Paget has been always most kind to me, *most* kind," said Miss Mortimer, with dignity.

"Yes, perhaps she has been kind to you," said Honor. "I don't deny it, but she doesn't like you. Yes, I *do* know, auntie, because you know I went up with her to your room when she came this morning before luncheon. You remember you said to me, 'Take Lady Hervey-Paget up to my room, darling, and ring for Rosine.' I did ring for Rosine," Honor went on, "but no Rosine came; and Lady Hervey-Paget took off her little cape and her veil, and then she looked at herself in the glass and she said, 'Dear me, what a fright I do look!' I said to her, 'Yes, you do.'"

"You never did!" cried Miss Mortimer.

" Yes, auntie, I did. It is always rude to contra-
dict people ; surely you know that ? Why, you have
told me so yourself many a time."

" Yes, dear, but not—not on such an occasion as
that. What did she say ?"

" She looked at me," Honor went on, " and she
said, ' H'm, you are a sharp-tongued little person.
Then, if you think I look a fright, miss,' "—the tone
was Lady Hervey-Paget's to the life,—" ' pray, tell
me what is amiss with me.' "

" And did you ?" asked Miss Mortimer, in a voice
of agony.

" Yes, auntie, of course, I did. I thought she
wanted to know."

" What did you say ?"

" Well, I told her," said Honor, rather unwillingly,
" that she had got smuts under her eyes."

" Smuts under her eyes !" repeated Miss Mortimer.

" Yes, auntie, all along ; they looked horrid. And
so she looked at herself in the glass hard, and then
she said to me, ' H'm, you have a quick eye, child,'
and she pulled a little case out of her pocket and
took out of it a queer little thing, not exactly a
brush and not exactly a pad, a sort of a little stick
covered with wash-leather—oh, so funny—and she
began to dab her eyes with it ; and then she took out
a little pencil and marked the dirty places all over
again ; and then she looked at herself in the glass

for a long time, and she said, 'I think that's better.'
And then she felt in her pocket again, and she said,
'Oh, dear, dear, dear! Where does your aunt keep
her colour, child?' 'Her colour,' I said; 'what
colour, Lady Hervey-Paget?' 'Why, her *rouge*, of
course,'" she answered.

Miss Mortimer gave a little scream. She was not
without vanities in that line, but she had, up to that
moment, believed them to be successfully concealed
from the inquisitive eyes of her nieces and nephews.
"And what did you say?" she enquired, quite
sharply.

"I told her I didn't know; that I didn't think
you had any colour; but she rummaged about in
your dressing-case and she found it; and then she
coloured herself up again and she said,—well, I
don't think I had better tell you what she said."

"Yes, tell me everything," said Miss Mortimer, in
a tone of deep tragedy.

"Well," said Honor, rather unwillingly, "she said,
'H'm! Aumonier's best rouge, a guinea a box.
Think of that ridiculous woman being so extrava-
gant as that!'"

"She said so to you?" repeated Miss Mortimer,
incredulously.

"No, she didn't say so to me," returned Honor;
"she said it to herself; and when she turned around
and saw me there, she said, 'Oh, run away, child;

run away, child. Children should never come spying about their elders.' I wasn't spying about,"
said Honor, in disgusted tones; "I didn't want to
see the old cat daubing herself up."

"Honor, my dear!"

"Well, it is true, auntie; I didn't. And she *is* an
old cat, auntie; and I thought it was horrid of her
to use your colour and then call you a ridiculous
creature. You are not half as ridiculous as she is."

"My dear," said Miss Mortimer, pulling herself
together with an effort, "I feel quite sure that Lady
Hervey-Paget, who has known me all my life, dear,
since I was a little girl no bigger than yourself,
would never speak of me in such terms. You must
have misunderstood her, darling, or she was speaking of somebody else. Sometimes old ladies have
a habit of talking aloud, and do not always intend
what they say to be taken literally. As for the
colour, darling, I keep it,—well, in case of accidents.
You remember the day that Tom and Georgie got
us into such trouble over the hurdy-gurdy man and
the monkey? Well, it was most useful to be able
to give dear Lady Camdentown a little touch of
colour, just to prevent people seeing how frightened
and upset she was. But as a regular use, dear,—
well, I don't know that I altogether approve of it
for that."

"Such as Lady Hervey-Paget leaving her own

colour behind," suggested Honor, plamping out the truth without the smallest attempt at impressing it as fiction, as Miss Mortimer had done.

"Well, dear, well, you won't talk about it, will you? Don't tell the others. It is a subject which ladies never talk about in public."

"Very well, auntie, I will say nothing about it, not even to Ernestine. I am sure," she went on, with a great sigh and an ominous break in her voice, "that I am very sorry if I have vexed you, auntie. I never want to do it. I begin to think that it is true what Crystal says, that it is a thousand pities we were not brought up to tell lies like other people."

"Does Crystal say that?"

"Oh, yes, often and often. I suppose," she added, a moment later, "that the minister at Fynlan was right when he told father that his plan would never work. It doesn't work to say just what's true. Mr. Duncan was right enough, and yet, why do these clergymen in England make all their sermons about truth-telling? They say, ever so plainly, that we are to do it; to keep on, no matter what the consequences are; but they do not tell the truth themselves; and they do not like it when other people do. I think, auntie," she said, with a deep sigh, "that living in England is just twice as hard as living in dear Fynlan."

" Well, dear," said Miss Mortimer, "perhaps it is
so. Strange things are always more hard than those
that we are used to, but by and by you will grow
accustomed to it, as Ernestine has done, and then
you will find life in England quite easy, probably
much easier than life used to be in your island home.
And you will promise me, dear, never to speak to
Lady Hervey-Paget again about her teeth or her
appearance in any way, darling. Unless you have
something very nice to say to people of their looks,
it is better always to avoid personalities in conversation. Of course, if you think any one looking very
well, or extremely pretty or very bright, it conveys
a compliment to tell them so, always providing that
one is not fulsome in doing so, but to mention teeth
to any one who obviously has false teeth——"

" I don't think I quite understand what obviously
means," said Honor, looking at her aunt with wide-
open eyes.

" Well, dear, obvious means apparent, easy to see,
something about which you can make no mistake.
Nobody could look at Lady Hervey-Paget and not
know in a moment that her teeth have been put in
by a dentist, that they are not actually growing in
her mouth. Do you see ?"

" Oh, yes, I see," said Honor,

" So, if you fancied any one had a wig, you should
never speak of wigs. It is always best to be on the

safe side in such matters, darling. That is just all the difference between good manners and awkward ones. There is not the slightest reason to tell other than the truth. Telling the truth—I mean to say being truthful—does not consist in being rude. You know a person may have a broken nose, and it would be the truth to say 'Your nose is broken,' but it would be very rude and very unkind. It would not be a lie to avoid speaking of broken noses. Now, do you see the distinction ?"

. "Yes, I think I do," said Honor, "I think I do. I will try, auntie."

"I am sure you will, darling."

Miss Mortimer felt quite relieved in her mind, for, though difficult, her young nieces and nephews were strictly honourable in all their ideas. For a few days after this little conversation, she saw that Honor was indeed trying hard to please her in every way, and her kind heart was quite touched by the child's evident wish to satisfy her.

Shortly after this, the family at the Chase became extremely busy, owing to a great festivity which was to take place in the park and the gardens. From time immemorial, or, if not quite so long as that, ever since such an institution had been known in West Brettleford, the Cottage Flower Show of the village had been held at the Chase. This year, as the family were in residence, Miss Mortimer determined to iden-

i

tify herself and her nieces and nephews with the
great village *fête* as much as was possible. To
further this end, she invited a very large house party
for the Flower Show week, as many people, indeed,
as the Chase would hold. She also proposed to give
a large luncheon party on each of the three days
that the Flower Show continued, practically to all
persons who chose to come for it, and to end up
each day's proceedings by a cold supper, of which
she intended to ask anybody personally known to
her to partake. In short, she determined to keep
open house, to restore the old traditions of the house
when it had been noted far and wide as one of the
most hospitable mansions in the entire county. So
there was great excitement in every department.
There was much scurrying to and fro between the
house and the railway station, much planning and
contriving, much ordering of stores and procuring
of extra help of all kinds, and at last, on the first
day of the Flower Show, which was to be opened at
three o'clock in the afternoon, a very large party was
gathered together in Miss Mortimer's drawing-room
as the clock was nearing the hour of two. There
was the great lady who was to open the show, there
was the bishop and the high sheriff, and such a
gathering of county magnates as had not been assembled within the walls of the old Chase for many
and many a year; and just as Miss Mortimer was

looking for the admirable James to come blandly in
and announce that lunch was ready, the wife of the
high sheriff created somewhat of a sensation by
slipping quietly back among the cushions of the
couch upon which she was sitting in a sudden
swoon.

In a moment all was confusion. One gentleman
ran for brandy, another for water, Ernestine was
despatched for smelling salts, and happily the great
lady was soon brought back to her senses, and
struggled to her ownself again with a thousand
apologies for being so inconsiderate as to faint upon
such an occasion. " I think," she said, feebly, " that
it was the fierce sun beating down upon the carriage
as we drove along. Ah, Miss Mortimer, I cannot
express my contrition——"

" My dear Lady Garrowby," exclaimed Miss Mortimer, " pray, don't let that trouble you for an instant.
I am sure nobody would faint if they could help it.
So long as you are feeling better, nothing else matters.
Would you rather not go in to lunch ? Shall I have
lunch sent in here ? And will you lie on the sofa, or
will you go and lie on my bed ?"

" Oh, no ; it is quite gone off. I shall be quite myself in five minutes," cried Lady Garrowby, who,
although a delicate woman, had a horror of making
a scene of any kind. " I am really all right. If I
had thought of it, and had asked your servant for a

little brandy as soon as I came in, this would never have happened. Indeed, you need not be in the least anxious about me; need she, Garrowby?"

" Oh, no; my wife knows herself thoroughly," said the high sheriff, who had been vigorously chafing one of his wife's hands. " Have a little more of this brandy, my dear, and you will be all right."

" But Lady Garrowby does look very pale," said Miss Mortimer, anxiously.

At this moment Honor electrified the entire assembly by a suggestion, which she made in all good faith, with the view of materially assisting the situation. " Shall I fetch Lady Garrowby a little of your colour, auntie?" she asked, in her clear high voice.

A sound which was something between a laugh and a gasp ran through the large company. Honor went on speaking, without giving Miss Mortimer time to say anything. " We keep a little colour by us," she said, in the tone of one anxious to communicate the exact truth. " Auntie does not approve of using colour as a regular thing, but, sometimes, when people are taken ill, it is very useful to make them look a little better. It is very good colour; it costs a guinea a box."

At this point, Ernestine, full of pity for the agonized expression of her aunt's countenance, intervened with as thumping a fib as any young lady ever brought to the rescue of an exceedingly awk-

ward moment. " Nonsense, Honor," she said, sharply,
" don't talk about things you don't understand. You
can't have private theatricals without *rouge;* and if
you do know that auntie gave some to a lady one
day when she was taken ill, you should not tell anybody. Of course, Lady Garrowby doesn't want any
colour, everybody knows she has just fainted. Really,
Honor, if you have nothing more sensible than that
to say, you had better hold your tongue."

And then, mercifully, James announced that
luncheon was served, and apparently the little incident was forgotten.

CHAPTER XII.

AMONG the guests whom Miss Mortimer invited to the Chase for the Flower Show week was her dear friend, Lady Camdentown, who, if the truth be told, had accepted the invitation with some misgivings, and who, indeed, took an opportunity of making her wishes very clear to the younger members of the family as soon as she arrived at her destination.

" Now, my dear children," she said, when she first made her appearance in the drawing-room, where afternoon tea was awaiting her, "there is nothing like beginning as we mean to go on, and for the sake of my comfort and your aunt's comfort, and in fact for the comfort of everybody concerned, I want to ask you to do me a great favour."

" Of course, Lady Camdentown," cried the four youngsters, with one breath. Ernestine was not included in the lecturette.

" Well, first of all, I want to ask you not to bring any monkeys here."

" No, no, of course not! As if we would!" exclaimed Sir Thomas, indignantly.

" No, no, of course not; it would be the most

134

unlikely thing for you to do, my dear boy; that I know perfectly well," Lady Camdentown said, with a jolly laugh. "But forewarned is forearmed, my dear boy, and whilst I am here we will have no monkeys, no hurdy-gurdy men or any of their clan, and, if you don't very much mind, we won't have anything of the surprise order. I have a great horror of surprises. It seems to me that your aunt has got her house inordinately full, and that everybody will have to be extremely good or else things will go wrong. Now, I intend to be remarkably good myself, and I am sure it will be a great deal easier for Miss Mortimer and everybody else if you make a similar resolution; and, my dear children, if you do happen to see things which were not intended for you to see, I would try not to talk about them."

"What sort of things, Lady Camdentown?" Sir Thomas asked.

"Well, my dear boy, for instance, if you happen to notice some one——"

"Whose teeth are like castanets," put in Crystal.

"Castanets? What does the child mean?"

"Oh, nothing, nothing," cried Honor, who did not want that subject to be brought up again. "I made a mistake once, that was all, but," with a crushing glance of scorn, "it was such an *obvious* mistake that there is no real fun in talking about it."

"Such an obvious mistake," repeated Lady Camdentown. "Bless me, what language these little chicks do use! But it is a very good word, Honor, an excellent word, and when you see anybody who obviously would rather not have certain things talked about, don't talk about them. Goodness knows," she went on in a confidential tone to Miss Mortimer, "I am as little touchy about my adjuncts as most people."

"And what are adjuncts?" enquired Honor.

"Adjuncts, my dear child? Oh, well, you will know one of these days better than I can explain it to you. Miss Mortimer knows quite well what I mean. And, as I was saying, I am as little touchy about my adjuncts as most women, but it is embarrassing, to say the least of it, to sometimes have a spade called quite a spade, and, so as to make me quite comfortable during my visit here, I hope that you will leave my personalities severely alone.'"

For a moment the four young Mortimers stared at her in amazement. Then Crystal all at once grasped her meaning and made haste to reassure her. "Why, Lady Camdentown," she said, in a suddenly comprehensive tone, "we wouldn't vex you for all the world, of course, we wouldn't. I didn't see what you meant for a minute. You see what it is, boys and Honor," she went on, addressing her brothers and young sister, " while Lady Camdentown is here we are not to talk about her scal——"

"Yes, that is exactly it," interrupted Lady Camdentown, drily, and putting out a warning hand to stop the rest of the objectionable word, "nor anything else of the same kind. Now, we understand each other thoroughly well, I am quite sure we shall be the very best of friends."

"Those are perfectly charming children, my dear," she remarked presently to Miss Mortimer, when the children had all gone trooping out into the gardens, "but they must be a terrible trial to you."

"You see," said Miss Mortimer, apologetically, "I have never been used to children."

"And such children!" returned Lady Camdentown. "However, there is one alleviating circumstance, my dear Elinor; they are good-looking, and, in spite of their appalling bringing-up, they are wellbred. Of course, if they *meant* the dreadful things they say, they would be intolerable, but their mistakes are obviously only the result of their appalling training. What an uncomfortable time your brother must have had of it!"

"I believe not," said Miss Mortimer. "I believe that my brother was perfectly happy in his extraordinary beliefs. I never could stand either him or my sister-in-law, Lady Muriel, at any price. I never quarrelled with them, you know, my dear; I never quarrelled with them. I never do quarrel with people, more especially with relations, but,

somehow, our lives lay apart. It was better so. I
have no sympathy with cranks. I am a woman of
few fads; I live the ordinary life of a woman of the
world, and peculiarities are highly objectionable to
me. I thought, when I first heard the news of
Thomas's death, that it was a dreadful thing that he
should be taken away, leaving five children orphans
at their tender age, but I have come to see that the
ways of Providence are merciful. They might have
turned out charming, as Ernestine has done, but I
am afraid that the probabilities are very much
against it. With boys, a more ordinary bringing-up
is I am sure much better. Ernestine has always had
the responsibility of feeling that she was the eldest,
the house-mother so to speak, and that and her
natural good sense have all tended for good in the
formation of her character. Crystal is more difficult;
Honor more difficult still. As for the boys, they
would have become impossible long before Thomas
had made up his mind to send them to a public
school."

"I think that you are right," said Lady Camdentown; "yes, I think that you are quite right, Elinor.
Providence does arrange things very well, on the
whole. Now with regard to Ernestine, she is
charming."

"Oh, Ernestine is everything that my heart could
desire, and endowed with more every-day common

sense than the others. Ernestine is quite reasonably worldly. As soon as she reached London, she saw at once the folly of carrying her father's ideas too far."

" She ought to marry well, for she is very pretty," said Lady Camdentown.

" I consider that she is lovely," said Miss Mortimer, in a tone of genuine affection.

" You are anxious, of course, that she should marry well?"

" Oh, yes; because on Ernestine's marriage most probably depends the marriage of her sisters. And she should marry well; she has everything which should bring about a good marriage."

" I suppose her *dot* will be something considerable?"

" They have each twenty-five thousand pounds on their marriage if it is with my consent, or on the day that they come of age," replied Miss Mortimer. " But Ernestine will probably have a good deal more. I am exceedingly fond of her. If she marries to my liking, I shall certainly increase her fortune."

Lady Camdentown edged her chair a trifle nearer to that of her hostess. They were quite alone together, all the other house-guests being out and about the gardens. " Elinor," she said, half hesitatingly, " what do you think of Dalston?"

" Of your son?"

"Yes."

Miss Mortimer looked at Lady Camdentown inquiringly. "As a husband for my niece?"

"Yes."

"But is he thinking of it? Has he any such idea?"

"Well, I don't think that he has," Lady Camdentown admitted. "I know that he thinks her extremely pretty, more than pretty; he told me so several times during the season, and he asked me the other day whether I meant to invite you to stay with us this autumn. I am a little anxious about Dalston, it is time that he settled down. Of course, it would be a great position for her."

"I don't undervalue that," said Miss Mortimer, slowly, "but Lord Dalston is,—well, it is just possible that Ernestine might not like him. I don't know that I should raise any objections to such a match,—not to his position, of course, dear Lady Camdentown, but he has been a little—a little——"

"Dalston has been very wild," said Lady Camdentown, in quite as outspoken a way as even the young Mortimers could have desired; "but then they, my dear, always make the best husbands. I am sure when I married Camdentown, the people all talked as if I were marrying—oh, well, as if I were running dreadful risks; but a better husband than he has been it would have been impossible to find. I have had my own way in everything ever since I was

married, and, and, after all, what can a woman have more
than that? For myself, I should be thankful if
Dalston did take a fancy to Ernestine. She is so
pretty, so well-bred, and I am fond of her. I confess
that, much as I should like my eldest son to marry, I
should like him to marry someone that would be pleasing to me personally; and, really, nowadays there is
always the dread of one's sons, particularly one's
eldest son, being carried off by some music-hall
creature, or some painter's model, or—worse. So
far as money goes, that is not a consideration. That
Ernestine has such a comfortable *dot* is, of course,
very desirable, very pleasant; but Ernestine herself
is far more precious to me than any fortune she
might bring."

"Well, I can say nothing," said Miss Mortimer;
"I should not attempt to force my niece in any way.
I think interference with marriage a dreadful thing.
If the young people,—I mean, if it came about naturally, I should not object; but I could not do anything
to help it on. I should not like to do anything to
help it on."

"But you will bring her to Dalston Towers during
September?" said Lady Camdentown.

"Oh, yes," returned Miss Mortimer; "I will bring
her to Dalston Towers with pleasure, but you quite
understand that I should not like to bias her in any
way."

" Oh, no! my dear, no! But if it came about it would be pleasant to both of us," said Lady Camdentown, in her easiest manner.

If the truth be told, Miss Mortimer was not altogether easy in her mind on the subject. Lord Dalston was the heir to a marquisate, he could make his bride a countess, he was very rich, and he was young, but he had the reputation of being exceedingly dissolute. True, his father had enjoyed a similar reputation before him, and Lady Camdentown had just said that he had made her an excellent husband. She certainly seemed as happy as the day was long, and Miss Mortimer had an idea that she was the last woman in the world who would trouble herself to make-believe on such a matter. However, although she was pleased and flattered at the prospect of such an alliance being held out to Ernestine, Miss Mortimer did not trouble herself any further about it just then. For one thing, her house was very full, and her time more than occupied. Lord Dalston was not to the front, and it was a matter which she could, for the present, leave very comfortably to take care of itself.

Meantime, Ernestine, in all unconsciousness of the little arrangements that were being planned out for her, was extremely busy in trying to help her aunt to make everything connected with the Flower Show go well and smoothly. Having been to all intents

and purposes for several years mistress of Fynlan
Castle, she was in her element when helping to su-
perintend the arrangements for a large number of
guests. If it had not been for her continual anxiety
as to the little ones, Ernestine would that week have
been perfectly happy. As it was, the dread of what
they might say or do was enough to keep her always
on the rack of apprehension.

At this time she was looking lovely. The exquisite fairness of her skin had become finer and clearer
in the gentler atmosphere in which she had been
living since her father's death ; her tall, slender figure
was slightly rounder in outline, and her anxieties
added to rather than took from the dignified charm
of her manner. It is safe to say that not one single
visitor to the Chase came during that busy week
who did not admire the young daughter of the house
more than anything else in it. In London, Ernestine
had had admirers by the dozen ; she had been ac-
counted one of the prettiest *débutantes* of the season.
At West Brettleford she was considered the beauty
of the neighbourhood.

It was Father Delamere, when he came down
again for the Flower Show week, who first pointed
out to Miss Mortimer that her niece had one admirer
who could not, by any stretch of the imagination, be
considered a desirable or suitable match for her.
" I suppose," he said to his hostess, one morning,

"that you have ideas as to your niece's marriage?"

"My niece's marriage? My niece is not going to be married," ejaculated Miss Mortimer, in a scared tone.

"No, no, not now; but in time to come."

"Oh, well, I should like her to marry suitably; I should like her to make a good marriage, of course. What woman, placed in my position, would not do so? But there is time enough, vicar, time enough."

"I don't know so much about that," said the vicar, drily. "She has one admirer down here who is very desperately in love with her, and I almost fancy you would not be pleased by the fact."

"And who is that?"

"The curate here, Jones."

"Oh, nonsense!"

"It may be nonsense to you, but it is no matter of nonsense to him," said Father Delamere, promptly. "I fancied last night that you did not see what was going on."

"*Nothing* is going on," said Miss Mortimer, in a very sharp tone.

"No, no, not between them; I saw that for myself. But something is going on in his mind, and he is as desperately in love as ever a young fellow was in this world. I have given you a hint, and you must see to the rest for yourself."

"I am sure, vicar," said Miss Mortimer, "I am very much obliged to you. Of course, I have not a word to say against Mr. Jones. I am sure he is a most estimable young man, but I do not think that he is quite a match for Ernestine; and, if he were, I do not think that Ernestine would ever care for him."

The vicar's hint was, however, enough to make Miss Mortimer distinctly uneasy, and she took the earliest opportunity of sounding Ernestine on the subject. Ernestine's laugh, when she realized her aunt's meaning, was sufficient to allay all her fears. "I marry that funny little man! Oh, auntie, what an extraordinary idea! What can have put it into your head?" she exclaimed.

"Nothing, dear, nothing. I only fancied—you know young men are young men whether they wear red coats or black ones, and I thought it best to put you on your guard, dear. Girls cannot be too careful, especially when young men are about, and he does come here a great deal. It was only an idea that crossed my mind, darling. Perhaps it would have been better to have said nothing about it."

"Oh, my dear auntie, what matter can it make whether you speak of it or not?" Ernestine replied. "Why, if I were cast upon a desert island, and there were not another man in all my world, I don't think I could bring myself to look at Mr. Jones,—in that light, I mean."

It soon became very clear to Miss Mortimer that Mr. Jones did not share Ernestine's opinion. He looked at her, poor fellow, often enough, much too often for his own piece of mind, and in her anxiety to make sure that Mr. Jones did not have too many opportunities of ingratiating himself with Ernestine, Miss Mortimer quite forgot to keep an eye upon a much more dangerous person.

CHAPTER XIII.

A TINGE OF WORLDLINESS.

THE more Miss Mortimer thought about Lady Camdentown's hint, the more enamoured did she become of the idea that her favourite niece might one day be Marchioness of Camdentown, and the more often she looked at her niece, the more convinced did she become that she had been born into the world wholly and solely that she might fill that particular position. Just at first, that is to say, for a few hours after her little confidential chat with Lady Camdentown, she had recalled, with a certain sense of uneasiness, the many objectionable things which she had heard from time to time about the young man. But she soon began smoothing down his little moral excrescences in the way a real worldly woman will. After all, young men will be young men, her thoughts ran, and if he *had* broken all the gas-lamps in South Audley Street, well, that was a venial offence enough. He might have done a great many things that were much worse. He was young, and boys will be boys. There was that affair about the confectioner's shop in Brighton,—yes, that *was*

rather disgraceful, and it seemed hard for her somewhat precise mind to see where the fun could be to
two young men, moving in the highest circles of life,
in going into a tart-shop and deliberately pelting the
passers-by with the contents of the window; but
then, although such conduct was foolish, it was not
more than foolish, nobody could say that. As for
his latest escapade, when he and young Lord Win-
dleston contrived to convey a couple of live geese
into Covent Garden while an opera was actually
going on, that was quite unpardonable. She herself
had been almost frightened to death that night, and
she had lost one of her best diamond hair-pins. Oh,
certainly, it was high time that such exuberant
spirits were toned down, and that Lord Dalston was
make a quiet and respectable member of society.
Personally, she rather liked him. Certainly he had
not his mother's dignity and charm of manner, but
then a wife like Ernestine would be the making of
him. Ernestine was so reliable, there was so little
of giddiness about her, she would be an excellent
steadier for a young man whose faults were the faults
of over-exuberant youth. And then, it would be a
great gratification to herself if her niece were to carry
off the best match of the season, and more particularly as she was an unmarried woman. Yes, it
would be a great feather in her cap, and Miss Mortimer determined that no help of hers should be

wanting to bring about such an exceedingly desirable consummation.

Several people who were present at that first great luncheon given for the opening of the Flower Show thought and said how exceedingly nice it was of Miss Mortimer to pay so much attention to the curate of the parish. The vicar was away, having been ordered a sea voyage for the benefit of his health, and Miss Mortimer had arranged that his representative, the curate, should sit very near to her. Of course, Miss Mortimer sat at the head of the table, and young Sir Thomas, with Lady Camdentown on one side of him and the wife of the high sheriff on the other, was opposite to her at the foot. "You are very young, my dear Tom," she said, "to have two such great ladies in your charge; but this is your house, and I wish you from the beginning to take your own position, as you will have to do later on. All I ask you to remember is that these ladies are your guests, and that you must neither do nor say anything which will make them uncomfortable or ill at ease."

To the unhappy little curate's supreme misery, Miss Mortimer singled him out for her especial favour that day, and told him to sit in a place which was only two removes from herself. Ernestine was on the same side of the table, much lower down, and when by leaning well forward he tried to catch a glimpse of her charming face, he found his vision each time intercepted by a manly shoulder and arm. And the worst of it was that he knew Ernestine was thoroughly enjoying herself; he knew that the owner of the shoulder and arm was paying her marked attention, and, poor little man, being very much in love himself, he was convinced that this man was in love with Ernestine also. As a matter of fact, Ernestine's companion was not in love with her so far. He had met her a week or so previously at an afternoon function in the neighbourhood,—an affair that was half garden-party, half dance. He had danced with her several times, had been introduced to Miss Mortimer, and had asked permission to come over to the Chase to call. He did call a couple of days later, had played a couple of sets of tennis with Ernestine, had feasted off tea and strawberries under the lime trees, and had impressed himself upon the mistress of the house as being a young man of unusually charming manners. He had then betaken himself back to his quarters again without in any sense conveying what an extremely dangerous young man he was.

" I think that is rather a pleasant young man, Ernestine," said Miss Mortimer, when he had bidden them adieu and they had watched his smart dog-cart go away down the avenue of copper beeches.

" Oh, yes, auntie, awfully nice," said Ernestine.

" He dances beautifully, and he really plays a very good game of tennis,—quite refreshing after those London men who cannot stand upright without the help of a doorway."

" I think," said Miss Mortimer, " that we will ask him to the opening lunch. Such a very presentable young man."

Eventually, Mr. Fitzroy was asked to the opening lunch, and quite by accident was the person to take Ernestine in. That came about in this wise : Just at the last minute Ernestine said to her aunt, " Auntie, dear, do manage so that that dreadful little man does not sit near me."

" What dreadful little man, darling ?"

" Mr. Jones. He is very estimable and very worthy, but he is so tiresome, and he does stare so. Do give him to somebody, so that he is obliged to be a long way off."

" Certainly, dear child. I will tell him that he must sit near me, and I will send him in with Lady Constance ; she likes a flavour of religion, per-haps because she is so worldly herself. And you had better go in with—let me see—Lord Gar-rowby ?"

" Oh, my dear auntie, please, no. Do give him to somebody nearer his own age,—some titled woman ; there are plenty of them. There is the bishop's wife, you know ; she must have a grand enough person provided for her. Let me have somebody a little young."

"Well, there is that nice young man who came over the other day from the barracks, Mr.—yes, Mr. Fitzroy. Let him take you in; he will amuse you very much."

"Then, will you tell him?"

"Oh, yes, dear, I will tell him to take charge of you."

Thus Laurence Fitzroy, with all the sanction of the powers that be, was sent in to luncheon with the fair young daughter of the house. He lost no opportunity of making the most of the situation, and Ernestine, in all ignorance that she was expected to one day become Marchioness of Camdentown, and exulting in the feeling that she was free even from the observation of the ridiculous little curate, gave herself up to the enjoyment of the moment and flirted as innocently and as heartily as any *débutante* ever did in all this wide world.

So far as her future peace of mind was concerned, that week of festivity was Ernestine's undoing. She awoke each morning with the sense that she was going to enjoy herself thoroughly; that life was fair, sweet, new, original, and charming. She looked forward with zest to every minute of the time, and each night when she went to bed she looked back with breathless satisfaction to the hours which were gone by. It was an idyllic time, such as only the very young and heart-whole can feel. With Ernestine it did not last long, because, when the Flower Show was come and gone, and all the big lunches and teas and suppers were over, she suddenly awoke to a sense that the world is not all bright. She suddenly became conscious of shadows in the picture and spots on the sun, of times when the sun did not shine at all, for, during the week following the Flower Show, she was bidden to a great festivity a few miles away, one of those gatherings which are only given in the country, when guests come from far and near, when bands are playing, marquees are erected, ices and fruit and scandal and "cups" of various kinds are the order of the day; and on this particular occasion, when Ernestine had donned her prettiest frock and her brightest smiles, there was no Laurence Fitzroy.

It is almost impossible to describe the girl's feelings when she realized that he was not present, that he was evidently not coming. A contingent of his brother officers arrived on the regimental coach—nine of them—but there was no Laurence Fitzroy. She wanted to ask where he was, but her lips refused their office. There was a little archery in one part of the grounds, tennis in another, croquet somewhere else,—there was even an Aunt Sally. She tried each and all of these elevating amusements, but they

were all stale, flat, and unprofitable. She danced
with several other officers of the regiment in a
marquee which had an excellent floor to the strains
of a perfect band; but it was no enjoyment to her;
there was no warmth in the sunshine, the light had
temporarily gone out. She could not imagine
why he had not come. He had told her distinctly
that he should be present on this particular occasion, but he had failed her, and Ernestine went
home feeling as old as Methuselah and as hopeless
as Job.

"You are very tired to-day, dear," said Miss Mortimer, marking her unusual quietude.

"My head aches a little, auntie," said Ernestine.
She flushed a fine, vivid scarlet as she spoke, for,
although she had become what might almost be
called worldly in comparison with the singular ab-
sence of worldliness in the Fynlan code of manners
and morals, she was yet sufficiently truthful of disposition to blush at having said something that was,
very wide of the real facts. In a measure it was
true, for she had a headache, but the headache was
not equal to the heartache, and she felt as if everybody else would know it.

It was not until three days later that she discovered the reason of Laurence Fitzroy's non-appearance
at Lady Garrowby's summer *fête*, when he rode over
to the Chase with the ostensible object of calling

upon its mistress. " I was so disappointed that I could not manage to get to Lady Garrowby's *fête,*" he told them; "and I hear it went off so very well, everybody enjoyed themselves enormously."

" It was quite a lovely party," said Ernestine, with distinct mendacity. " We all enjoyed ourselves tremendously much ; didn't we, auntie ?"

" Why," said Honor, staring at her sister with wide-open, round eyes, "you came back with an awful headache."

" Oh, yes ; I did have a headache," said Ernestine, flushing a fine and guilty scarlet again ; " but although I had a headache, it was a beautiful party ; everybody said so."

" I am sure it must have been," said Mr. Fitzroy, enjoying her discomfiture not a little, and inwardly deciding that he would make Honor a present before very long. Then he drew the child nearer to him, " And did you go to the *fête*, little woman ?" he asked. " I noticed that our colonel's two little girls went."

" No, only Ernestine went that day," said Honor. " We had a special *fête* of our own at home. We had ices for tea,—and grapes,—and hot-cakes. It was a funny mixture," she went on, enjoying his perplexed look; " yes, it was a funny mixture, wasn't it ? We chose it, you know, because we were not let to go to Lady Garrowby's *fête.*"

" Why weren't you let to go to Lady Garrowby's
fête ?" he inquired.

" Well, you see, we were asked," said Honor, in
confidential tones, and so occupied in looking at him
that she never saw the glances of warning cast at her
by Ernestine and Miss Mortimer; "oh, yes, we
were asked, of course, but auntie is so horribly afraid
of our telling the truth. We have a fatal habit
of telling the truth—all of us, excepting Ernestine."

" My *dear* Honor," put in Miss Mortimer, in a
tone of deep displeasure, " Mr. Fitzroy might think,
from your description, that your sister was in the
habit of telling deliberate untruths. You ought to
explain, if you persist in going into such details, that
you younger children have a really fatal habit of
always telling the blind truth, whether it is palatable
or unpalatable, whether it is polite or impolite,
whether it is kind or unkind."

" Dear auntie," said Honor, in a perfectly unabashed tone, " you heard Ernestine say for yourself
just now that she enjoyed Lady Garrowby's *fête*
awfully. She didn't enjoy Lady Garrowby's *fête* at
all. She came home with a splitting headache.
How could anybody with a splitting headache enjoy
a *fête* ? Besides that, Crystal asked her—I heard
her myself, with my own ears—if she had had a lovely
time, and Ernestine said, ' No; perfectly horrid.' I

don't know what *you* would call that; *I* call it distinct story-telling. I am quite sure father would have had a fit if he heard any one of us making such absolutely outrageous assertions."

"My dear child," said Miss Mortimer, in a tone of sharp disgust; "you don't understand what you are talking about"

For a moment there was blank silence. Then Ernestine, with a face like a flaming, fiery furnace, came to the rescue. "Honor doesn't understand, auntie," she said, with half-deprecating vexation. "I had a headache on the day of Lady Garrowby's party, but I did enjoy myself in a way. I enjoyed seeing other people enjoy themselves, and—and—it is very disagreeable to have one's words repeated in that way. You are very foolish, Honor."

"I cannot," said Honor, in a grand aside to the walls, or the pictures, to anything rather than to the assembled human beings, "I cannot understand things at all. The more I tell the truth, the more foolish I seem to be and the less understood by everybody. Everybody seems to understand lies. Servants say ladies are not at home when they are, when they know they are, and when we object to that we are told, 'Oh, but *every*body will understand.' Yet, whenever I tell the truth, everybody says, 'But you don't understand.' Upon my word,

it is most awkward, most difficult, to know what to
say."

" I think you had better go out into the garden,"
said Miss Mortimer, " and get some fruit or do something.   And don't try to understand what is beyond
you, my dear."

She heaved a great sigh of vexation as Honor
and Georgie betook themselves away.   " My dear
Mr. Fitzroy," she exclaimed, " I don't know what
you will think of those dreadful children.   Poor
lambs, they do not mean wrong, but they had an
extraordinary bringing-up, all of them."

At this point Ernestine slipped away, and Miss
Mortimer and Fitzroy were left alone in the drawing-
room.   " My poor brother was really a most estimable man; so single-hearted and so good, and so
cranky, Mr. Fitzroy, so cranky.   Do you know, I
quite blush for my own wickedness and my own—
well, shall I say my own-double-facedness whenever
I think of him.   He brought these poor lambs up
in a new creed, that they should tell the truth, the
whole truth, and nothing but the truth.   They were
not even allowed to suppress it occasionally, hence
this painful result.   Ernestine is like other sensible
girls of her age; she saw as soon as she came to me
in London, the inadvisability of blurting out unpleasant things and persisting that they must be
right because they were not untruths, but the little

ones are even more imbued with my brother's absurd notions than he was himself. We really are afraid to let them go about as much as we should do, because we never know what they will say next."

" But does it matter ?" he asked.

" Well, in a sense it does matter : it cannot always be explained, as to-day. Of course, the child made Ernestine uncomfortable for a moment, but she is so sweet that she will not remember it after a few minutes. Still, when old ladies get their top-knots discussed as scalps with perfect openness before a crowd of people, and when a child tells some one with the most palpably false teeth in the whole world that *now* she understands how some people's teeth rattle like castanets, it becomes very awkward for the guardian of those children. I cannot make the dear things see that Ernestine's saying that she had enjoyed Lady Garrowby's party when she really had a headache, is not telling an untruth. Why, I often say I have enjoyed myself when I have been simply bored to death, but I do not consider that I am actually guilty of telling lies. So trying it is. No? Won't you have another cup of tea? Oh, you had better."

" My dear lady," said Fitzroy, with a laugh, " when you consider the quantity of tea that I have had, I am sure, if you follow Honor's habit of telling the blind truth, you would say I had very much better not."

"Well, as you like, as you like, of course. Then would you like a game of tennis? If so, do go into the garden and find the others."

CHAPTER XIV.

HONOR FEELS DEEP SHAME.

FOR a wonder there were no visitors staying at the Chase, and Fitzroy went out with alacrity through the long French window and to that part of the gardens where he felt that it was most likely he might find Ernestine. He did not find her quite as easily as he expected, but when he did come across her he tabooed the idea of tennis, which she at once mooted. Not that she wished to play, poor child, but she proposed it simply as a cover for her intense nervousness.

"No, don't let us play tennis," he said; "it is so hot. At least, it isn't so hot, but it would be much nicer to walk around and look at things a little. Supposing you take me down that shrubbery,—you know, the one where we went the very first day that I ever came to the Chase. I have a tender memory of it. Let us go and see if it is as nice to-day as it was then."

She turned and walked back beside him, more because she could give no reason why she should not do so than from any other cause.

"If I mistake not," he said, "there is an arbour

in that shrubbery. Ah, yes, I thought as much,—a
nice clean, brick-built arbour which has apparently
just been done up. Don't you think," he went on,
drawing her into it by sheer force of magnetism,
"that this is an improvement on tennis? After all,
tennis is for people who haven't got the brains or
the interest to talk to each other; tennis is not for
you and me. One might play tennis and enjoy it
with the ugliest woman that God ever made."

In a moment the fun flashed back into Ernestine's
face again. "You might sit here and enjoy it with
the ugliest woman God ever made," she said, with a
delicious laugh.

"Ah, now you look like yourself again. That
little soul vexed you just now. Why did she vex
you?"

"Oh, she did not vex me—I—that is to say, I am
always vexed when she vexes auntie, because auntie
is so good to us, and we must be such a horrid
nuisance to her. Fancy a woman living a comfortably fixed life, on a comfortably fixed income, with
comfortably fixed habits, being suddenly boarded by
a host of savages as we were, and having all her life
altered, all her habits, ways, and customs literally
torn up by the roots and shoved into new ground to
take root again as best they could. I feel so sorry
for my aunt; I can hardly explain to you how much.
And she is so good to us, she never really reminds

us what a nuisance we are, not even when she feels it most."

" But *you* were never a nuisance to her ?"

" I don't think that I was, after the first few days. Of course, I was older than the others, and I realized from the very first what a difference we must make to her. Do you know, Mr. Fitzroy," she said, looking at him with her crystal-clear eyes, " that we all arrived in London, fresh from my father's funeral, dressed in tartans, dressed in outrageous tartans, like a horde of barbarians. Poor auntie, and she had gone into so much deeper mourning than she would otherwise have done, because she did not wish to hurt our feelings."

" But why did you ?"

" Because we had never heard of mourning in our lives,—we had never seen it. We had a band of crape round our arms, and that was all ; our knowledge of mourning went no deeper than that. I often think of the shock it must have been to poor auntie when she saw us drive up in the railway bus, with enough live-stock to fill a bazaar stall, and our island piper, who would call everything 'she.' Poor auntie!"

" What have you done with the piper now ?"

" Oh, he is here. Didn't you hear him all last week ?"

" Was that your own man ?"

" Of course it was. We couldn't understand people of position travelling without a piper, and, having
brought him, we felt that it would break his heart if
we were to send him away. But I have always the
dread that he will get drunk. He did get drunk
once," she said, naïvely, " and poor auntie was so
frightened."

" I am sure she was. I don't like a drunken man
myself," said Fitzroy, watching her with all his eyes.
" And now tell me, Miss Ernestine, and pray tell me
the truth, why didn't you enjoy Lady Garrowby's
fête ?"

" I don't know," said Ernestine ; " I didn't enjoy
it—much."

" You had a headache, of course. But what gave
you a headache ?"

" Oh, I cannot say." She turned her head somewhat away so that he could only see the edge of one
crimson cheek, the tip of one little pink ear.

" I was so disappointed that I could not get to it,"
he went on, in tones that were unmistakably genuine.
" I raged."

" But why ? Why did you not get there ?"

" Because I couldn't."

" But you promised that you would—at least, I
mean," trying to draw back, for she felt that she had
gone too far, " I mean that you said that you were
going."

" I had every intention of going ; but when a man is on duty, and everybody else wants to be going their own way, so that he cannot get a friend to take his duty for him, what is that man to do ? He must stay at home. And so did I, Miss Ernestine. I stayed at home, and I grizzled, and I wondered if you would notice that I was not there. I did not like to give a message to one of the other fellows ; I did not know what to do. I hoped that you would miss me. I thought possibly you might."

" I missed you dreadfully," said she.

" Oh, do you know I am glad that you missed me, dreadfully ?"

" Are you ?"

" Yes, I am very glad. I do not feel my disappointment half so much now."

Something came over Laurence Fitzroy that afternoon that, come what might, he must hear definitely from Ernestine Mortimer that she loved him. Right up to the day of Lady Garrowby's summer *fête* he had not been what is usually called " in love,"—at least, like her, he had not been aware of it. Somehow or other, during the long hours that he had been kept a prisoner in Rendlesham barracks, he had become alive to the fact that he was more than ordinarily annoyed at being kept a prisoner by the exigencies of duty ; and as he sat there that brilliant summer day in the clean and secluded arbour, a wild desire to possess her for his own came over him and blotted out every other feeling.

He was, however, doomed to disappointment on that particular day, for, just as he was about to tell her what she was certainly longing to hear, there was a sound of footsteps on the gravelled pathway without, and the next moment Honor and her two brothers came in at the doorway.

" Oh, Ernestine," cried Honor, "ever so many people have come to call, and auntie wants you to go into the drawing-room particularly."

Fitzroy fairly groaned. " Do you want to go in, Mr. Fitzroy ?" said Honor, fixing him with her brilliant eyes ; "you have had one tea, and you said then you couldn't eat another bit. Auntie gave us a broad hint to stop out ; she said there were too many people in the drawing-room already. Don't you think you had better stay out with us ?"

" Yes, I will stay with you," said he ; then went a step or two after Ernestine, who was already on her way to the house. " Miss Ernestine," he said, "you will come back, won't you ? I have something most particular to say to you. Won't you come back here as soon as you can get free ?"

" I can't get free until they go away," she said, looking at him, half nervously.

" Well, but when you are free. I will come in presently, if you are kept very long ; but they may go

away if they do not see other people here. Give
them a chance of doing so, won't you ?"

She nodded her reply and scurried away along the
shrubbery path. Fitzroy turned back into the
arbour where the three children were in possession.
" Now, why on earth didn't you say that you couldn't
find your sister ?" he said, vexedly.

" Because it would not have been true," replied
Georgie.

" We saw you come in here ever so long ago,"
chimed in young Sir Thomas.

" And we never tell lies if we can help it," said
Honor. " That is why auntie doesn't want us in the
drawing-room now. Auntie is dear and sweet and
everything that is nice and good," Honor went on,
beginning an elaborate explanation, " but she does
tell stories; and, really, I think Ernestine is worse
than she is. Of course, we are awfully fond of
Ernestine,—she is quite the dearest girl in the
world,—but I often think," with a great sigh, " that
if father could hear her say the things she does it
would be the very death of him. Mr. Fitzroy,
wouldn't you like to go round and see the stables ?"

" Very much, indeed," said Fitzroy, who saw by
this means a possibility of keeping out of the house
for the present.

So the four went along to the stables, where, as I
have said before, there was not very much to be

seen, or I should rather say that there was not very much in the way of horse-flesh to be found there. On this particular afternoon there was a good deal to be seen, and Fitzroy was edified by a nearer acquaintance with the Fynlan piper than he as yet had been honoured with, for the festive Tammas had taken the opportunity of spending a few of the " tips " which had been bestowed upon him during the course of the Flower Show the previous week; in other words, Tammas was drunk, and Tammas knew it.

Fitzroy and the youngsters arrived upon the scene in time to find the gigantic Scot holding on with might and main to the stable-pump, "She were no drunk," he remarked to the stable-lad, who was grinning delightedly; " no, she were no drunk. She had had a wee drappie ou aye, she had had a wee drappie, and her heid were a bit buzzing, but she were no drunk. And she were at Fynlan, she would be just sleeping among the hay and there would be no fuss whatever, but the mistress no ken the difference between a wee drappie and being sair drunk. So if ye'll just pump on her heid she will be herself in twa cracks."

The stable-boy, however, who dearly loved a joke and liked to keep the Fynlander on tenter-hooks, stood grinning, but never a pull at the pump-handle did he give. Twice did Tammas hold his head under the spout, and twice did he lose his balance and tumble into the muddy stone trough below, but, as soon as the two boys saw the true state of affairs, they made a simultaneous rush to displace the lad.

" Hang on to him, Geordie," cried Sir Thomas, " and I'll pump. Get out of the way, Ted."

In a minute young Geordie had flung himself, with the agility of a monkey, on to the Fynlander's broad back, and was holding his head well under the pump. Sir Thomas, hanging on to the handle, pulled with might and main. " Hold on, Geordie !" he cried.

" I am holding on," cried Geordie. " Pull away, Tom ; let h im have it. Keep your head under."

In vain did the spluttering, more-than-sobered piper howl for mercy. The lad, born and bred in the stern air of Fynlan, and having the piper wholly at a disadvantage, clung like a veritable Old Man of the Sea to his back, pressing his feet hard against the sides of the trough and holding his head well under the pump. Honor danced round the two, aiding and abetting in a perfectly shameless and scandalous manner by as neat a perversion of the truth as ever a truth-teller was guilty of. " Keep your head under, Tammas, Miss Ernestine's coming. Now, pray, keep your head under. Pump away, Tom. Hold him tight, Geordie." She, too, with all the agility of her unusual bringing-up, administered deft kicks now and again which completely floored the

H   15

unfortunate Tammas. And all the while, Fitzroy
and the stable-lad stood holding their very sides with
laughter, and Fitzroy even forgot his indignation at
the interruption which had come to him. It was not,
indeed, until the two boys' arms were aching and
refused to perform their office any longer that they
let their unfortunate victim go, and Tammas, spluttering vigorously, and looking like a half-drowned rat,
rose to his feet a free man once more.

" You had better cut," cried Sir Thomas, chafing
his hands hard together, " for, if Miss Ernestine
catches you, it will be good-bye to any more life in
England. On my word, Tammas, you ought to be
awfully obliged to us, you really ought. We did
better for you than Ted would have done. Why, I
should think you must be as sober as a judge."

" She is half drowned," cried the piper, ruefully.

" Yes ; but she isn't half drunk, Tammas," returned
the boy, with a burst of laughter. " Now, pray, get
along out of sight. We won't tell a soul."

" Unless," said Honor, " Ernestine or auntie should
happen to ask us. I am not going to tell stories
just to save Tammas, that I promise you."

" Miss Honor," said the more than half-indignant
piper, " ye didn't mind scaring her with the news that
Miss Ernestine was coming. She thought it was all
over with her ; yes, she did, indeed, whatever."

For a minute or two Honor stood still, appalled

by the enormity of the crime which had been brought home to her. She attempted no excuses; she knew that she had *not* expected Ernestine to be coming, that, in other words, she had strayed very far from those paths of truth in which she had been reared. " Tammas," she said, at last, " I am ashamed of myself. That was a downright thumping lie, Tammas, and I don't believe that I ever told a downright thumping lie in all my life before. It only shows," she said, looking with great solemn eyes at Fitzroy, " what a thing it is to live in a cataminating atmosphere. Tammas, I abjectly apologize to you."

I am bound to say that at this point Fitzroy went off into immoderate yells of laughter. He sat down upon the nearest seat which came to hand, which happened to be an antiquated horse-block, and laughed until he was positively ill.

" There is nothing to laugh at," said Honor, severely. " If you knew how ashamed of myself I feel, Mr. Fitzroy, you wouldn't laugh."

But Fitzroy evidently did not know, and he continued laughing most heartily until he was joined in a perfect chorus by the two boys and the recalcitrant Tammas, whose red locks and beard were still all aglitter with the tubbing bestowed upon him by his young masters. Only Honor kept her imperturbable gravity, and gazed from one to another with wide-open eyes filled with astonishment and displeasure. " I think," she said, deliberately, " that you ought all of you to be very much ashamed of yourselves, particularly Tammas. You have not only been drunk, which you know perfectly well is forbidden, but you have incited me to tell a downright lie," she remarked, addressing the still grinning Fynlander. " Perhaps one expects that sort of thing of boys, of boys who have not any father; but you are a man, a grown-up man, and you think it funny that this English gentleman should see you getting your head ducked to save you getting into a row with Miss Ernestine. I wonder, Tammas, that you are not too much ashamed to go on living."

" Indeed, Miss Honor," said Tammas, trying hard to repress his unseemly levity, " she was deeply ashamed of herself," and with a tug to his wet, crimson locks, Tammas made a sheer bolt of it.

CHAPTER XV.

THE BITTER RECOGNITION OF WORLDLINESS.

In due course of time the two boys went back to school, and the French governess, who was in charge of Honor and Crystal, returned from taking her holidays. Then Miss Mortimer was able to breathe freely once more, and it was with a heart very much inclined to count up her blessings that she set about her preparations for her visit to Dalston Towers. She insisted upon Ernestine having a couple of new white dresses, and also a couple of very pretty frocks to wear by daylight, and she had long consultations with Rosine, who prepared all sorts of pretty garments for the girl, to Ernestine's great satisfaction and pleasure.

It happened on the very day of their departure for Dalston Towers that Mr. Fitzroy rode over from Rendlesham to call at the Chase. The faithful James informed him, with the imperturbable air of a man accustomed to London, that his mistress was away from home.

"Oh, really? And have they all gone?"

"Only my mistress and Miss Ernestine, sir," replied James.

15*   173

" Then the other young ladies are at home ?"

" I believe that they are, sir," James replied.

" Do you know if they are in ?"

" I think not, sir. I believe the young ladies, with mam'zelle, are somewhere in the grounds."

" Well, I think I will just look over, as I have come so far," said Fitzroy. " I will take my horse round to the stables and stay for a little while."

" The young ladies are certain to be in at five o'clock, sir," said James.

" Ah, yes; then I will walk round and see if I can find them."

It was a long ride from Rendlesham barracks to the Chase without having any rest by the way, so Mr. Fitzroy put up his steed, and just as he was sauntering back in the direction of the western terrace, he found himself almost knocked over by a young lady with a gigantic hoop.

" Oh, is it you, Mr. Fitzroy?" cried Crystal. " You know auntie and Ernestine are away, don't you ?"

" So James has just told me, Miss Crystal," he replied. " But, you know, I thought, as I had come so far, that I would give my gee a little rest, and you and your young sister could tell me the news."

" Well, we have no news," said Crystal, turning and walking back beside him; " no news. Mademoiselle pricked her finger rather badly this morning. I think there is nothing else to tell you."

"And Miss Mortimer, she has gone away?"

"Yes, auntie has gone with Ernestine to Dalston Towers. That is Lady Camdentown's place, you know. They have gone for a week. Ernestine is very, very happy. She has got such a lot of new dresses, and she is going to have such a lovely time. I do envy her."

"Does she like Dalston Towers?"

"Oh, Ernestine has never been there," Crystal answered; "but she is very fond of Lady Camdentown, who has always been most kind to her. We are all fond of Lady Camdentown, every one of us. She is a great friend of auntie's, you know."

"Yes, I gathered as much. I daresay it is a very nice house to stay in. Your sister was very delighted to go?"

"Oh, yes," answered Crystal, unhesitatingly, "she was. It was very funny," she continued, with a gay burst of laughter, "but Tammas, our piper, you know, was so frightfully upset because he could not go, too, But auntie was firm, as firm as a rock. 'Nothing, my dear Ernestine,' was her comment, when she heard his wish, 'would induce me to go to any large country house with an incubus like Tammas hanging about me.' Tammas says that English people have no idea of their dignity, and he has

been more or less in the sulks ever since. I quite
expect," she ended, "that something will be happen-
ing."

"That Tammas will be throwing up his place and
going back to Scotland?"

"Tammas throw us over?" exclaimed Crystal,
with wide-open eyes, as clear as her name. "Oh, I
don't quite think so. Tammas is as fixed as the
stars in heaven. When my brother is old enough,
of course, Tammas will be attached to him, because
he is the head of the family; until then he will stick
to auntie. But auntie struck at taking him to Dalston Towers, of all places."

"Why, of all places? They have room enough
for any quantity of people, surely."

"Oh, yes; but did you never hear what happened
at the first party auntie gave after we were in
London?"

"No."

"Oh, I will tell you about it." And then she told
him the whole story of their escapade with the monkey, and the disastrous result to Lady Camdentown's
toilet. "She really was most extremely good about
it," Crystal said, when she had told the story in all
its nakedness, "because, you know, she might really
have cut us, and she might have cut auntie, which
would have been dreadful; indeed, a thousand unpleasant things might have come of it. Oh, yes, she

was very good, she really was; but, naturally, auntie wouldn't take Tammas to Dalston Towers."

They were joined then by the French lady and Honor. Crystal introduced Mr. Fitzroy to Mademoiselle, and explained to her how far he had come, and told her that she had asked him to remain to tea.

" I don't know," said Fitzroy, " whether I ought to do so; but it is rather a long ride to take without a break."

He spoke in excellent French, and the lady, so far from being shocked and playing prim propriety, bade him welcome as kindly and as cordially as Miss Mortimer herself could possibly have done. " You would like to have a game of tennis ?" she suggested. " These children simply love it; they have been all day wishing that somebody would come to relieve the monotony of their playing together."

" Do you not play yourself, mademoiselle ?" he enquired.

" No," she replied; " I do not find tennis agreeable to me. I am of a languid nature, and prefer, this hot weather, to sit under the trees and read or work."

She had a book in her hand at that moment, and she settled herself in a comfortable wicker-chair while the two girls and Fitzroy played a vigorous game of tennis, he against the pair of them. Then

James came out and told them that tea was served
in the morning-room, when they all went in and
made very merry over the little meal; after which
Honor invited Fitzroy to go and see her new kittens
before he took his departure.

While she was chatting with him, she made use
of the expression, "When Ernestine comes back
again," and Fitzroy rather caught at the words.
"And when is Miss Ernestine coming back?" he
asked.

"Oh, that we don't know,—in about a week.
You know," she said, looking at him with her big,
solemn eyes, "you know why they have gone?"

"On a visit."

"Well, not exactly that," said Honor; "at least,
they have gone on a visit; but they have gone really
to find out whether Ernestine would make a proper
sort of mistress for Dalston Towers or not."

"What?" cried Fitzroy.

"Yes, that is just it. I don't know what a mistress does at Dalston Towers, nor why they want
one, but I heard Lady Camdentown say to auntie,
one day, 'Ernestine would make a charming mistress for Dalston Towers,' and auntie said, 'Oh, well,
we shall see, we shall see.'"

Her tone was Miss Mortimer's to the very life, but
Fitzroy was too much upset by the news which her
innocent remarks conveyed to be amused at her

unconscious mimicry, as he would have been at any other time. They went on to the stables, where the cats were, Honor still holding forth at the top of her fresh young voice, but all the glory of the day had died for Laurence Fitzroy. He could not doubt the truth of the child's words; they bore its very own impress.

So Ernestine was going to be sacrificed, like so many other girls of her class, on the altar of position, for the religion of worldliness. He had thought this frank, fresh, fearless, ingenuous family were people who had stepped right out of the ordinary track; he had fancied that Miss Mortimer was something more than a mere match-maker. He knew Lord Dalston, knew him well; knew what a worthless, dissolute, idle, mischievous life his had always been; but Ernestine had been tricked out in new gowns and other garments, and had been taken off to stand her trial, as it were, to see if she would be good enough to suit the taste of this young Pasha, this lordling puppy, whom he despised with all his heart and soul. And Ernestine had been glad to go. No wonder, if she had had that in her mind, that he had never had a chance of saying the word which he had hoped and believed would be all that was necessary to make her his forever. That was at the bottom of everything, and the deepest sting of all lay in the fact that Ernestine had gone willingly

CHAPTER XVI.

MEANTIME Miss Mortimer and Ernestine had duly arrived at Dalston Towers. They found the huge mansion extremely full and the party a very large one, and, not a little to Miss Mortimer's satisfaction, the eldest son of the house, from the moment of their arrival, paid Ernestine the closest and most marked attention. Never before had Miss Mortimer so worried about Ernestine's looks as she did on that first evening while she was dressing for dinner. She herself superintended the details of her toilet, fussing in and out of her room, and harrying Rosine with hints and suggestions in a wholly unusual way.

"Dear auntie," said Ernestine, suddenly becoming aware of the unusual fussiness of her aunt's manner, "why are you so anxious about me to-night of all nights? Rosine will turn me out looking all right. Why are you worrying so, dear?"

"Well, darling child," returned Miss Mortimer, with a distinct perversion of the truth, such as ought to have made the late Sir Thomas turn in his grave, "this is the first time that you have ever stayed in a very large house, and I am most anxious that you should make a good impression, especially on this your first evening."

" Why, you are more anxious than ever you have been in town. Even for the Drawing-Room you were not so fussy as you are now," Ernestine cried, laughingly.

" So long as the result is all right, a little fuss is well spent," replied Miss Mortimer, with quite a sententious air.

The result in this particular instance was to make Ernestine look absolutely charming; and when she went into the drawing-room in her aunt's wake, Lord Dalston, who was lounging near to the door, jumped up and immediately attached himself to her. " I believe, Miss Ernestine," he said, " that I am to have the honour of taking you in to dinner. Do say that you are glad, because so many times one has to take people in to dinner to whom one is absolutely indifferent,—who, in fact, bore one to death."

" I hope I shall not bore you to death," replied Ernestine, ignoring the question as to whether she was glad or sorry. " I do not think I generally have that effect upon people. I might, you know, but it is not likely. What is much more likely is that you will bore me."

She laughed as she spoke, and looked at him with her clear, lovely eyes. She was quite unconscious of anything approaching to coquetry, and Dalston

admired her more than ever, and thought her the
very loveliest creature that he had ever seen in his
life. As a rule, this young man had not been much
attracted by girls of Ernestine's type, but he had
always promised himself that when he married it
should be to a woman of his own class. Up to the
present time he had not given marriage a thought,
except as something that was as inevitable as that
one day we must all die. He had passed most of
his life, since the completion of his education in London, associating with ladies in whom refinement was
not the most predominant characteristic. Like many
other young men of his acquaintance—"Johnnies"
was the actual term that he would have used—he
had a most familiar acquaintance with the various
ladies who exhibited themselves at the music-halls,
and he might have been seen any night gazing with
a fatuous expression, and vacant eyes indicative of
anything but amusement, at the various Japanese,
Indian, or fancy ballets which happened to be running at the time. He knew every fashionable bar-
maid in London, and generally spoke of a young
lady as a "little filly." Ernestine, of course, did not
recognise him for what he was, simply because she
had no intimate knowledge of his type; but, although
he took the utmost pains to make a good impression
on her, her only feeling was that it was a pity Lord
Dalston was not as charming as Mr. Fitzroy.

If the truth be told, Ernestine had not been so overjoyed at leaving the Chase as her two young sisters had believed. She had taken an interest in her clothes just as any other young girl would have done under similar circumstances, but she had not gone to Dalston Towers expecting to have an especially brilliant time of enjoyment; in fact, she had rather looked forward to being one of the least important of a very smart party. It was an instinct which made her feign deeper interest in that particular visit than she really felt. In truth, she was a good deal puzzled by the fact that Mr. Fitzroy had never spoken the words which she felt were in his heart. She was very young, but she was possessed of all the best womanly instincts, and it was indomitable pride which made her hide from her little world something which was not quite a wound, a hurt which was most of anything like an accidental bruise, which pained her, nevertheless. For Lord Dalston and all his kind she had the most profound and unmitigated contempt, as was but natural with a girl who had been brought up among a simple, hardy, and exceedingly manly people. In London she had thought him a poor enough creature, in the country she realized one shortcoming after another with a wonder which, if the young man himself had but realized it, would surely have stung him into amending his entire habits of life with new ones.

Now, it happened that the very first morning after
their arrival, Ernestine heard from Rosine that Miss
Mortimer was not feeling particularly well, and as
soon as she was dressed, she went into her aunt's
room to see what was amiss. "It is nothing very
much, dear child," said Miss Mortimer, in answer to
her tender solicitude ; "a little headache, dear, that
is all. Don't you trouble about me. Rosine will
see that I get a little breakfast. I shall be all right
by lunch-time. Do you go down, dear, and get out
into the fresh air. You will see, darling, what Lady
Camdentown suggests for the morning. Of course,
the men will all be off shooting. Perhaps there will
be a lunch, and some of the ladies will walk with the
guns, but do you do what will amuse you, and what
you think will please Lady Camdentown."

Thus empowered to use her own discretion, Ernestine went down to breakfast. She was one of the
earliest to reach the great dining-room. Soon after
her came her hostess, who was at all times an early
riser, and three or four other ladies, mostly those
who had what may oe called morning complexions,
straggled down one by one. She found that there
was to be a big lunch at a certain spot, about five
miles from the Towers, and Lady Camdentown made
a list of those who wished to join it.

"Now, I would clearly have you all understand,"
she said, "that nobody need go who prefers to eat

their lunch on this table instead, for there will be lunch here at the usual time; but I have promised to go myself. I do not join shooting-lunches very often, but I have promised to go to-day. Ernestine, my dear child, would you like to go or not?"

"I should like to go very much, thank you, Lady Camdentown," replied Ernestine, who was not beyond the age of taking a hearty interest in everything that she did.

"And your aunt, my dear; do you think she will go?"

"I don't think she will; she is not very well this morning. I fancy not."

"If she is not very well, she had much better stay at home and have lunch quietly here, more particularly as we have a rather large dinner and dance to-night. Then you will go. Lady Alleyne, do you intend to go?"

"Oh, yes, Lady Camdentown, I would like to go, thanks. I love shooting-lunches; they are immense fun."

"And your sister, will she go?"

"Oh, I am sure she will, thank you."

"Mrs. Egerton, you will go, won't you?"

Mrs. Egerton replied that she would be delighted to do so, and very soon Lady Camdentown's list was complete. "We will start at twelve o'clock," she said. "If those who are going will be ready in the

16*

court-yard punctually at twelve o'clock, we shall not
keep the men waiting. Until then, I will leave you
all to your own devices. Most of you know the
ways of the house and the various points of interest.
Mudie's newest books are in the library, the tennis
lawns are in perfect condition, and I hope you will
all make yourselves very much at home until twelve
o'clock."

" Ernestine, my dear child," said Lady Camdentown, half an hour later, when they had both finished
breakfast, " what are you going to do ?"

" I am going up-stairs to see if auntie is better,"
replied Ernestine.

" And then ?"

" Then I would like to go into the gardens and
look about generally. Please, don't trouble about
me ; I shall be perfectly happy until twelve o'clock."

" Will you ?" a little doubtfully. " You are quite
sure ?"

" Oh, yes ; I am quite sure," Ernestine replied.

" Then I shall see you at twelve o'clock," said her
hostess. " I am always rather busy in the mornings,
for I have naturally a good deal to look after ; and
this morning I must go down to the vicarage to
attend a meeting,—merely a little parish matter, but
one which I must not neglect."

" Don't give me a thought," said Ernestine.

And so with a laugh and a kindly pat from the

elder lady to the girl they parted. She learned from
Rosine that Miss Mortimer had fallen asleep again,
so, feeling perfectly happy on that score, she put on
a sailor-hat and went off into the gardens by herself.
And they *were* gardens. Ernestine had never seen
anything like them before. She wandered here and
there, up and down, in and out, admiring and noticing
everything, and, if the truth be told, thinking a little
of that absent one whose conduct was such a mystery
to her. She knew that he cared for her; what woman
ever does remain in ignorance when a man's whole
heart is beating in unison with hers? Certainly not
Ernestine Mortimer, who was as yet entirely un-
spoiled by touch with the world. Yes, she knew
that he cared for her. I think I may say that she
gloried in it; but she could not imagine why he
had never spoken; why he had never told her so.
Surely, her thoughts ran, as she paced up and down
among the alleys of an old-fashioned garden which
had been laid out entirely with a view to the cultiva-
tion of the sense of smell, he must know perfectly
well that she cared for him. She had never tried to
hide it from him; she had been glad at his coming;
sorry at his going; always happy in his company.
He was so stalwart, and yet, no, that was not the
word; he was such a man, so wiry, so full of endur-
ance, so fresh and frank and honest; he was a gentleman without being superfine, fastidious without being

ridiculous. He was unlike all these men that she
met about in every-day life, these men who called
themselves " Johnnies," these creatures who——

" Good-mornin', Miss Ernestine," said a voice behind her.

She turned round with a start. There was the
very person in the flesh whose type she had been
describing in the spirit. Lord Dalston, dressed in
light summer flannels and wearing a straw hat upon
his head, was standing holding out his hand.

It gave Ernestine quite a shock. " Oh, Lord
Dalston," she said, " how you startled me. I never
heard your footsteps on the gravel."

" No," he replied, in a slow drawl; " I shouldn't
think you would, because I walked on the turf. I
was just goin' to say a 'penny for your thoughts,
Miss Ernestine.' What were you thinkin' of?"

" I don't think that my thoughts would particularly
interest you, Lord Dalston," said Ernestine, promptly;
" at all events, it would not interest me to tell them.
How is it you have not gone shooting with the
other men ?"

" Not good enough," he replied, eyeing her up
and down approvingly. " All these chaps, they are
so uncommonly keen about shootin', that I thought
it would be a pity to take away so much as a single
shot from them. I can shoot, you know, and I do
sometimes, but I don't think it is worth the price,

myself. Have you been into the hot-houses and the conservatories?"

"No, I haven't," said Ernestine; "but I have been nearly round the gardens."

"Oh, the gardens are not interestin', and the sun's so blisterin'. Come along into the conservatories, they are awf'ly jolly. If we stay out here we shall find some ultra-energetic party who wants to nobble us for tennis. Do you ever play tennis, Miss Ernestine?"

"Oh, yes, indeed I do," said Ernestine, promptly.

"Oh, do you? I never do. Life's too short to play tennis. You don't want to play tennis this mornin', do you?"

"Oh, no; I am quite willing to go into the conservatories," replied Ernestine, speaking with the most heart-whole sense of enjoyment. "I love conservatories. I don't think people who have them make half enough of them. I always told auntie so at the Chase."

"Are the conservatories good at the Chase?" he asked.

"Well, yes, they are very good, indeed; but they have not been kept up as they would have been if my people had lived there always. My father, you know, hated the Chase because my mother was never well there, somehow. At Fynlan, our conservatories were not anything out of the common. We have

them, and I used to take intense interest in them,
but they are not like the conservatories at the
Chase."

As she spoke they reached the path which led
down towards the long string of conservatories which
ran along the entire length of one great wing of the
house. "Now there's one of these houses which
has somethin' like a decent temperature," Lord
Dalston remarked; "it is where they keep the birds.
Supposin' we make for that? It is one of the few
places round about the Towers where one can spend
a mornin' very profitably."

"But," said Ernestine, "I have promised your
mother that I will be in the court-yard at twelve
o'clock."

"Really? And what are you goin' to do in the
court-yard at twelve o'clock?"

"I am going with the others to the shooting-
lunch."

"Oh, you are goin' out with them, are you? I
wouldn't, if I were you. Supposin' we stay here and
have lunch by ourselves?"

"What? in the conservatories?" cried Ernestine.

"No, not in the conservatories,—in the house."

"Oh, no," she cried; "I promised to go with your
mother."

"I don't know," said Lord Dalston, in a half-
grumbling tone, "why ladies want always to go with

the guns. They get in the way, they waste time, and they get a bad lunch,—half earwigs. If we hadn't got a big dinin'-room, we shouldn't be satisfied. As it is, the main aim and object of my mother's life is to get out of it on any excuse whatever. Then you don't feel inclined to give it up?"

"Oh, I cannot," said Ernestine. "Why, Lady Camdentown might be very much annoyed. I should throw all her plans out."

"I don't think that she would mind," said Lord Dalston, who was perfectly well aware of his mother's desire that he should amend his ways and settle down into a state of high-class respectability. "I don't think she'd mind a bit, if you wanted to stop, that is. Anyway, I ain't goin' to be done out of my mornin' with you. So, if you have made up your mind, Miss Ernestine, to go to the shootin'-lunch, I shall go, too."

CHAPTER XVII.

CLEARING THE WAY.

IT would be hard to say by what accident it happened that Ernestine never told Miss Mortimer anything of her real feeling for Lord Dalston ; yet it is a
fact that she never did so, and Miss Mortimer, who
was not a little elated by the position of affairs, went
away from Dalston Towers perfectly happy in the
assurance that her niece was on the eve of making
the most important marriage just then possible to
her. The many advantages of such a marriage
were constantly present with her, and no one of them
was, perhaps, more continually in her mind than the
deference and attention which she herself received as
the aunt and guardian of the young man's probable
bride. To women of Miss Mortimer's world, to
whom even money is not everything, a title, such as
he bore and such as he was heir to, is like a cloak, it
covereth a multitude of sins, sins both of omission
and of commission. It would have been almost like
the utterance of a blasphemy to Miss Mortimer if anyone had told her that Lord Dalston was an ignorant,
vacuous, brainless creature, that he was dissolute,
worthless, almost invertebrate, that to sacrifice a

fresh young girl like Ernestine, whose bright mind
was far above the average both of her sex and class,
to the arms of such a husband would be an iniquitous
and wicked thing, she would only have felt that her
informant was a person dominated by some feeling
of personal spite against Lord Dalston or herself.
He was quite devoted to Ernestine. He did everything to show her honour, with the exception of
getting up early in the morning, and even on that
point he made her a sort of an apology for his
remissness.

"By Jove! you know, a fellow can't burn the
candle at both ends, Miss Ernestine," he remarked
one day, when she was half playfully reproaching
him with having carried his town habits into the
fresh country; "no, by Jove! I really can't get up
early in the mornin'. It's so uncomfortable, don't
you know. I like the world to get warm before I
have to do with it. All very well about the early
bird, you know; but what about the early worm?
Always thought the early worm an awful little duffer
myself to go and get gobbled up when he might
have been perfectly safe by stayin' in bed a bit
longer."

"Nobody wants to gobble you up, Lord Dalston,"
cried Ernestine.

"Don't they, Miss Ernestine? Ah, I think you
are wrong there. At all events, I can't get up early

in the mornin'. I don't like it, and it doesn't like
me, and, as I said just now, it don't do to burn the
candle at both ends."

"Then why do you burn it at the other end?"
asked Ernestine, severely.

"The other end? Well, one don't much here,
you know. By Jove! there's little chance when you
ladies have gone to bed of burnin' the candle at all.
Some of us do have a little flutter of a night, the last
thing; what else is there to do in the country?"

"Why, go to bed, of course," said Ernestine, with
a gay laugh.

"Only, unfortunately, we are none of us in the
hahit of goin' to bed early in the evenin'," he replied, seriously. "By the bye, do you know that
Miss Mortimer has asked me to come and stay a few
days at the Chase with you?"

"You don't mean it? Oh, I didn't know that
auntie was going to have another house party."

"Perhaps she isn't. She has asked me, anyway,
and I am comin'. I want to see the Chase aw-
f'ly."

"Oh, it is not much of a place," cried Ernestine,
"nothing to this. And my two young sisters will
tease the life out of you. It is a lucky thing for you
the boys have gone back to school. I wonder now
what my aunt asked you to come to the Chase for?
You will certainly be bored to death. Poor auntie,

she means to be kind to you, I am sure; but she doesn't know what she has let herself in for."

" Miss Ernestine, I shall not be bored," he said, in a tone of conviction just dashed with tenderness.

" I am not so sure of it," returned Ernestine.

" Auntie," she said that evening, when they had retired for the night, "you have asked Lord Dalston to come to the Chase ?"

" Yes, dear," said Miss Mortimer, sweetly.

" Dear auntie, why did you ?   He will be bored to death.   There is nothing there to amuse him."

" Oh, I don't think he will be bored, dear child," said Miss Mortimer.

" Don't you ? I do. There is nothing there for him. I really do wish that you hadn't asked him. Are you going to have a house party ?"

" Well, I thought one or two people, dear. Of course, one couldn't ask a young man quite by himself; that would be too pronounced altogether. I thought we would ask one or two,—Lady Constance, and perhaps Mrs. Valpé; they are great friends, and I am very fond of both of them; and then I must ask Colonel Stretton, of course, and I thought I might ask Sir Charles Bonner."

" Just those ?" said Ernestine, in a tone which was distinctly one of disappointment.

" Yes, dear. I couldn't do with a large party again. They do involve so much trouble."

" Oh, well, as you like, auntie ; but I am quite sure that Lord Dalston will be bored to death."

" I think not, darling child," said Miss Mortimer, in her kindest tones. " Dear child," her thoughts ran, as Ernestine betook herself to her own chamber, " she evidently has no idea that Dalston is desperately in love with her, and how much nicer it is when girls do not know. Somehow, I felt from the first day that the dear child was going to be a great comfort to me. I only hope the others will turn out like her. I am afraid not, I am much afraid not. Dear children they are, of course, all very sweet and dear ; but they have not Ernestine's comprehension of life. She has grasped the question of life just in the right way and just far enough. It is a great comfort to me that Ernestine should be as she is. Dear child !" and then Miss Mortimer, from the long force of habit, knelt down and said her prayers, among them that one which says, " Lead us not into temptation, but deliver us from evil."

CHAPTER XVIII.

LORD DALSTON arrived at the Chase rather late in the afternoon of a lovely September day. He was the first of the small house party to put in an appearance, Miss Mortimer having judiciously arranged that he should spend one evening *en famille* with them before the arrival of her other guests.

The weather was warm and balmy, and the beautiful old house lay bathed in the rich mellow light which you only get in this country during the month of September. The thought which struck him first was that the castle at Fynlan must indeed be very large, since Ernestine could speak of the Chase as being a mere nothing; his next was that Ernestine's sisters were two of the handsomest children he had ever seen in his life. They happened to be returning from some private little excursion of their own just as the carriage, which had been sent to fetch him from the station, emerged from the avenue of copper beeches and passed along the west wing towards the front of the house. The two girls, in their smart country suits of brown tweed, with

bright scarlet Tam-O'Shanter bonnets set jauntily
upon the masses of their sunny hair, reached the
principal entrance just as the carriage stopped. He
knew at a glance, from their likeness to Ernestine,
that they were the younger daughters of the house.

"How d'y do?" he remarked, with the easy famil-
iarity which is one of the trade-marks of the modern
"Johnnie." "I see that you are Miss Ernestine's
sisters."

"Yes, we are Ernestine's sisters, and you are
Lord Dalston," replied Crystal, promptly. "We
know you are Lord Dalston, because nobody else is
coming to-day. Why did you come a whole day
before the others?" she demanded.

"Why? I suppose because I was asked," he replied. "For my part, I am very glad that I have
come a day before anyone else; it will help us to
get better acquainted with each other."

"Yes, we may get to know each other better,"
returned Crystal, eyeing him with the unflattering
gaze of a still uncorrupt childhood. "Do you like
tennis?" she asked.

"I think," interposed Honor, "that we had better
go in and ask those questions later on. Auntie will
certainly be vexed if we keep Lord Dalston standing
on the doorstep."

Lord Dalston turned to her quite gratefully.
"Yes, indeed, Miss—Miss——"

" My name is Honor," she said, by way of helping him out.

" Ah, yes. Miss Honor; charmin' name, charmin' name. By Jove! it suits its wearer. As I was sayin', it's rough luck for a fellow to be kept on the doorstep, particularly when he has been asked to come in. By Jove! Miss Honor, you help a fellow out wonderfully."

It was the first time in her life that Honor had ever been treated quite as a grown-up young lady. She took to the new order of things with avidity. " Come this way," she said, with quite a grown-up air; " James will look after your things. I suppose my aunt is in the drawing-room, James?"

" I believe Miss Mortimer is in the drawing-room, Miss Honor," replied James, leading the way. The faithful servitor had no idea of having his work taken out of his hands by one of what, in the privacy of his own heart, he was accustomed to call " them young savages from Fynlan." " This way, my lord," he added, to Dalston. Honor felt the snub, and felt, too, with that innate love of the truth which was in her, that she had almost broken her promise to her aunt that she would never in any way interfere with the execution of James's duties. She, therefore, did not keep up with him quite as she would have done if James had remained to look after the new visitor's belongings. Crystal, who was

troubled by no such thoughts, on the contrary
increased her step with a hop, skip, and a jump.
" My name," she announced in a shrill voice, which
had no touch of shyness about it, " my name is
Crystal. Do you think my name suits me ?"

" Perfectly," said Lord Dalston ; " admirably."

They were walking down the long corridor leading to the drawing-room. It was one of the handsomest points of the very handsome house, being
wide and lofty and completely lined with show-cases
containing a vast collection of different porcelains.
As it was lighted from the top, she had no difficulty
in seeing him well, and she gave utterance to the
thought which was passing in her mind with an un-
hesitating frankness which ought to have put Lord
Dalston upon his guard. " I believe," she said, deliberately, " that you are making fun of me."

" Upon my soul, I wasn't," ·he replied, which was
not true. " I think it is the prettiest name I have
ever known in my life. What made your people call
you by it ?"

His apparent earnestness almost deceived her, but
she still looked at him a little doubtfully as they
walked along side by side. " My people gave it to
me for a reason," she replied, still half on her guard
against the only weapon of which she had any
dread, the weapon of ridicule; " but I don't think it
is a pretty name, and I don't believe that you do. It

is a name with a purpose, but it isn't pretty. We were all given our names with a purpose," she continued, "excepting Tom—my brother, you know. He was called Thomas because the eldest son of the Mortimers has been Thomas forever. Ernestine—Honor—and Crystal, that's what we are called, and Geordie is called George Washington, after the man who could not tell a lie, you know."

"Why, you don't mean to say," exclaimed Lord Dalston, stopping short and regarding Honor with eyes of the utmost astonishment, "that the Mortimers are Quakers, or anythin' of that kind?"

"I don't know what Quakers are," said Honor. "Auntie goes to church, and we go to church with her, but dear father was a Truth-teller—— What did you say, Lord Dalston?" she enquired sharply, the next moment.

"Nothin', nothin'. It doesn't signify," he said, hurriedly.

What he had said, in truth, was "Good God!" and, unfortunately for him, Honor had heard it. "You said 'Good God!'" she remarked, in a tone of much severity. "How you can call that nothing, I do not know. I call it a very great deal to say."

"Well, I did; but I didn't intend you to hear it," said he, hurriedly. Then as James opened the drawing-room door, added in an undertone, "You must tell me more about the Truth-tellers to-morrow."

In the drawing-room he found Miss Mortimer and
Ernestine.   Miss Mortimer was judiciously glad in
receiving her visitor.   She was much too well-bred
a woman, and, if the truth be told, much too experienced in worldly matters to let him see how intensely gratified she was by his acceptance of her
hospitality.

"I suppose," she said to him graciously, when he
had taken Ernestine's hand and was feasting his
eyes upon her fresh loveliness, "I suppose it is no
use offering you any tea, as it is so near dinner-
time?"

"Thanks, no; I never drink tea," was his prompt
reply.

"Well, for other things, I must leave you to
James's tender mercies," said Miss Mortimer, graciously.

At this moment, Honor, having edged nearer to
him, fixed him with her speaking eyes and asked
him a direct question.   "Don't you ever drink tea?"
she asked.

"No, not very often."

"Oh! and why don't you?"

"Because I don't care for it," said Lord Dalston.
"Men don't often drink tea."

"Besides," put in Miss Mortimer, "we do not
wish Lord Dalston to drink anything that he does
not like."

"Oh, no, no, certainly not, auntie, but I wanted to know why he doesn't like it," persisted Honor.

"For one thing," he replied, "because tea is extremely bad for the nerves."

"And do you have nerves?" the child asked. Her tone was one of such unmitigated contempt that even Dalston, who was as thick-skinned as a rhinoceros, could not but wince under the thought that was implied.

"Don't worry Lord Dalston, my dear child," said Miss Mortimer, coming hurriedly to the rescue.

"But I wanted to know, auntie," exclaimed Honor, pathetically.

"Never mind; don't tease, dear."

Thus admonished, Honor relapsed into silence, but she kept her shining eyes fixed upon Lord Dalston's vacuous countenance, much to that young gentleman's discomfort and dismay. He was quite glad when the dressing-bell rang. "By Jove!" his thoughts ran, as he brushed his hair before the flower-decked dressing-glass, "she told me they would tease my life out, but I didn't think she meant in that way. What on earth can they have been thinkin' of to bring up children to blurt out just what is in their mind as those two young ones do? I should think the old girl knew a trick worth two of that. Thank goodness, Ernestine's got more sense. Truth-tellers, indeed! I wonder what Truth-tellers are. Somethin' like Plymouth brothers, I should fancy."

"Miss Ernestine," he asked, later in the evening, when dinner was safely over and they were in the drawing-room once more, "are you a Truth-teller?"

"Well, I hope I always tell the truth, Lord Dalston," Ernestine replied, smiling at him.

"No, but I mean this—your young sister told me just as I came in that your father was a Truth-teller. What does that mean?"

"Well, it means exactly what Honor says. My father and mother had—I do not like to call it a craze, because it sounds like a reflection on their characters, and they were very good people,—but they had a crank for telling the truth, and they made that quality their entire religion, and we have been taught that as long as you tell the absolute truth you cannot go wrong. It did very well in Fynlan, where everybody had to give way to us, and we set the fashion so to speak, but out in the world it is most awkward, and I am really learning to tell what Honor would call lies quite prettily."

"That's a blessed relief," was Dalston's fervent comment.

"I told you they would tease you to death," Ernestine said, laughing at his perturbed look; "they will give you no mercy; they will give you no peace. I advise you to get up to nine o'clock breakfast. You will never hear the last of it, if you don't."

" Nine o'clock breakfast!" he repeated, as if she had advised him to rise and perform his orisons at break of day. " By Jove! you know, Miss Ernestine, a fellow would be so deadly done up before dinner-time."

"Oh, no; for we cannot stay up very late here; and you cannot stay up very late by yourself; that would be too dull. I really advise you, particularly the first morning, to make an effort and get down to ordinary breakfast. You will find it worth it in what it will save you."

" But why does your aunt let 'em talk like that? Particularly the little one, Crystal."

" Well, poor dear auntie is most anxious to prevent Crystal from ever talking at all, as she generally contrives to let her truth shafts fly with such deadly precision that every one makes a bull's-eye. But Honor is an irrepressible young person, and she will have her say. She will have it all out with you about your nerves yet."

A few minutes later, when Ernestine had gone to the piano to play something, Miss Mortimer took the opportunity of smoothing away any awkward corners that might be jutting out in what Dalston was pleased to call his mind. " My dear Lord Dalston," she said, in confidential and yet indulgent

18

accents, "I hope you won't let that dear child, Honor, worry you too much. She is the most dear child in the world, but my poor brother's children have had such an unfortunate bringing-up in some ways that it makes their society a little difficult. Believe me, it is the wisest not to answer her questions too fully. Put her off a little; I find that is the best of anything."

For a moment Lord Dalston struggled between his desire to say bluntly that Honor was the most forward brat that he had ever known in his life and to make a good impression upon Ernestine's guardian. Prudence, however, won the day, and he made haste to reply. "Oh, Miss Mortimer, don't trouble about me. I am pretty thick-skinned, and if it pleases the young lady to ask me a few questions, by all means let her ask them. I have nothin' to hide. I don't like tea, and I do think it's bad for the nerves, and I don't drink it, but, really, I don't mind the whole world knowin'."

Miss Mortimer gave a sigh. "They will ask you fifty such questions during the course of to-morrow," she said, half vexedly. "Not so much Crystal, she is getting more sensible every day, but Honor,—oh, Lord Dalston, I assure you the fertility of that child's imagination and the ingenuity of her mind are the greatest trials of my life."

"Never mind, Miss Mortimer," he exclaimed,

quite gallantly, for him; "don't put yourself out
about it. I can stand as much cross-questionin' as
most people."

"Now, are you going to take my advice," Ernestine asked, as she bade him good-night, "and get up
to breakfast to-morrow? Remember, it is my last
word to you. If you value your peace of mind for
the next few days, be down to breakfast at nine
o'clock to-morrow morning. You will be grateful
to me some day for it."

In view of his little conversation with Miss Mortimer, and the foretaste he had already had of
Honor's curious cast of mind, Lord Dalston felt that
there was wisdom in her words. "Miss Ernestine,"
he said, in a preternaturally solemn voice, "I promise you; yes, by Jove! I absolutely promise you that
I will be down to-morrow mornin' before the clock
strikes nine."

CHAPTER XIX.

THE REAL AND THE WOULD-BE.

By a violent effort, Lord Dalston did manage to reach the breakfast-room before the clock struck nine on the first morning of his stay at the Chase.

" Why," cried Ernestine, when she first perceived him, " you have really done it ? Well, I congratulate you. I assure you it will be worth it in the long run."

" I didn't do it for that," said Lord Dalston ; " I did it because you asked me. By Jove ! I'd do a good deal more than that for you, Miss Ernestine."

" Would you, really ?" cried Ernestine. " Why, you are getting quite a knight-errant ! But beware how you make rash promises ; and tell me, don't you feel rather proud of yourself ?"

" I don't," said Lord Dalston, as frankly as even the late Sir Thomas could have wished. " I feel as if it were the middle of the night ; and I hope that you will reward me after breakfast by takin' me all round the place and showin' me everything. I suppose your young sisters will be busy with their governess."

She could not help laughing outright to see how

heavily her young sisters were weighing upon his mind. " Oh, yes, they will be safely out of the road during a greater part of the day. You know, you must not let Honor victimize you. She is really a very dear child, but she has a habit of victimizing quite innocent and well-intentioned people. We were brought up so absurdly—but here they come. I will tell you about it afterwards."

The next moment the rest of the family came in almost together, mademoiselle with the two girls, and Miss Mortimer a couple of minutes later.

She greeted Lord Dalston with much kindness, enquired how he had slept, and asked him with an indulgent air what he would like to do before luncheon.

Lord Dalston was a young gentleman who never sacrificed his inclinations to other people if he could possibly help it. " Oh, well, thank you very much," he said, promptly; "but Miss Ernestine has undertaken to provide for me this mornin'."

" Oh, really? And what are you going to do?" the lady of the house enquired.

" We are goin' to explore the place. There is nothin' I love so much, Miss Mortimer, as loafin', doin' absolutely nothin', potterin' about. On my word, it is the best life out, especially for the first part of the day."

The voice of Honor broke in with relentless and

pitiless distinctness. "Some of these days," she said, in a terribly clear voice, "you will know what it is to want those hours that you have wasted in loafing."

"Bless my soul!" remarked Lord Dalston, turning his startled eyes like a pair of boiled gooseberries upon the child, "what did you say?"

"I said you would live to want those hours, Lord Dalston," Honor replied. "At least, that is what mademoiselle is always telling me; and I don't spend time doing nothing, not ever. When I have got a little time to myself, I spend it in reasonable play. Mademoiselle calls that waste of time; and she says, too, that one hour in the morning is worth two at night. I wonder what she would say to the way you throw your hours away."

Dalston was weak enough to attempt to argue the point. "But I am not wastin' my time, Honor," he said, mildly. "I couldn't," with a little bow towards Ernestine, "possibly be wastin' my time when I am cultivatin' your sister's acquaintance."

"Cultivating my sister's acquaintance!" repeated Honor. "What, and are you going to cultivate Ernestine? What are you going to cultivate her in? Tennis?"

"I don't think we are goin' to play tennis," said Lord Dalston, with something like a stammer in his tones.

"Oh, don't you like tennis?"-

"I don't care for it."

"Oh! Then are you going to play croquet?"

"I don't quite think so."

"Oh! You are going for a ride, perhaps?"

"I don't think that was a part of our programme."

"Then what *are* you going to do?"

"Your sister is goin' to show me the place."

"Oh! Do you mean that Ernestine is going to show you the walls of the house, and the shrubs in the gardens, and the flowers, and the asparagus beds, and so on? How very peculiar. I wonder," she said, with unconscious irony, "whether you or Ernestine will be the better for it."

"I hope," said Lord Dalston, with a look at Ernestine, "we shall both be the better for it."

"Well, I don't believe Ernestine will," was Honor's comment, "because showing you a house that she knows by heart, cannot possibly do her any good."

"She will feel that she has done me good," he suggested.

"Yes, she may. Perhaps that would be a satisfaction to her."

"My dear Honor, I am sure you are getting quite out of your depth," cried Miss Mortimer torn between a desire not to snub the child and a wish that she could be persuaded by any kindly means into absolute silence.

The astute French woman who had charge of the

two girls, and who knew fairly well the position of affairs at that moment in the household, saw by the agonized look on Miss Mortimer's face that the remarks of the over-truthful Honor were becoming unbearable. "Come, my children," she remarked, in her native tongue, "you do not seem to know that we are distinctly late this morning. Come, come. Miss Mortimer will, I am sure, excuse us."

"Mademoiselle!" exclaimed Honor, in a tone of shocked surprise, "look at that clock."

"Yes, yes, my dear, I do look at the clock; but it is a little wrong."

"The dining-room clock in this house is never wrong," said Honor. "I have never heard you question it before. At all events, we sat down to breakfast at nine o'clock to the minute, and we were going by that clock."

"Come, come," said mademoiselle, "don't argue the point. It is enough that I tell you that we are already a little late." She arose and hustled Honor cleverly out of the room.

"I don't care, mademoiselle," they heard the shrill, childish voice cry in expostulation, "I will speak; you may frown as much as you like, but that clock is not late, and you knew it was not; that is telling a story, mademoiselle."

For a moment Miss Mortimer knew not whether to be vexed or not. Then her gaze fell upon Ernestine, who simply sat back in her chair and laughed helplessly. "Oh, auntie, auntie! That poor child, that unfortunate child, she will be the death of you one of these days!"

"Does she always keep you on the grid like this, Miss Ernestine?" inquired Dalston, looking up from his third egg with a perfectly stolid countenance.

"Always," answered Ernestine. "Honor is a dear child, Lord Dalston, but she is like an accusing conscience; she is like the monitor of one's soul. My father used to call her the little angel of truth; but oh, dear, dear, although little angels of truth are very well at Fynlan, they are trying when they get into the outer world. I read a story the other day about an angel who got lost, got out of heaven and couldn't get back again, because her wings were wet, or she was moulting, or something, and she was so inconvenient to everybody. And that's what I feel about Honor. She is so inconvenient."

"It is the most difficult part of my whole life," said Miss Mortimer, gently, yet with a very decided sigh; "it is impossible to be angry with the child merely because she tells the truth, especially when we all know that we ought all of us to live such lives that we can always hear the whole truth told without flinching. Unfortunately, few or none of us do live such lives, and mine at present is passed in an atmosphere of dread for fear of the amount of truth that Honor will tell. Really, Lord Dalston, you must forgive me that I did not put you off until this evening. You see, you are interesting to the children because you are a new-comer, and therefore all Honor's attention is concentrated on you."

"Oh, it doesn't matter, Miss Mortimer, I am pretty thick-skinned," he replied.

It was quite true, and the declaration of this particular characteristic was a favourite expression with this young sprig of nobility; at the same time, a resolve formed itself in his mind much more quickly than his thoughts and resolutions were accustomed to come. It was that if ever he should find himself Honor Mortimer's brother-in-law, he would give the young lady a very wide berth so far as staying in the same house was concerned. However, the *enfant terrible* being safe in the fast keeping of the school-room and mademoiselle, Dalston determined that he would make hay and way with Ernestine while the sun shone.

In due course of time, their peregrinations brought them to the arbour where she and Laurence Fitzroy had spent one brief but never-to-be-forgotten spell of time on the day when she had first realized, or fancied that she realized, that he cared for her. "Ah, now this is a jolly place," was his well satisfied remark. "Supposin' that we sit here and rest ourselves, Miss Ernestine. I am sure we've walked miles since breakfast time."

" Yes, but I don't think we will sit and rest here," she said, hurriedly. "It is not a very nice place, and I would rather not sit here."

" Why not? It is so clean and sheltered. It is an ideal summer-house."

" No, no, I really cannot sit there," said Ernestine. " It is earwiggy."

" But it is all so clean," he persisted. " Ah, do come in, and we can have a nice little confidential talk."

" No," said Ernestine, " I don't want a confidential talk—at least, I couldn't enjoy a confidential talk there, not in that summer-house. You mustn't ask me. Really, believe me, I know what I am talking about. Don't ask me to sit in that summer-house, Lord Dalston."

" But why not? It seems so—so—just the very thing. Why shouldn't you come in and sit there a little while ?"

" I don't know why," said Ernestine, desperately. " I only know that I couldn't, that I would rather not," and she began resolutely walking away along the shrubbery pathway, so that Dalston had no choice but to follow after.

She hurried along at such a rate, her eyes shining and her cheeks flaming, that it was as much as Dalston could do to keep up with her. " I say, Miss Ernestine," he said, almost dejectedly, " do you think that we need go in for a walkin' match? Because, you know, it is rather early in the day to try that sort of thing, and, really, we have been walkin' for miles. Couldn't we sit down somewhere or other?"

She turned and looked at him, then laughed. " Why, yes, of course, I am very inconsiderate; but I didn't want to sit in that particular summer-house,—that was all,—and I hate being persuaded against my will to do anything. I have not yet shown you the south garden, where the sun-dial is. There is a sort of arbour there that is too delightful, all quaint old shells stuck into the walls, with rustic seats, and a curious pebbled floor. I don't believe you have ever seen anything like it."

She moderated her pace and led the way to the south garden. It was the quaintest bit in all the beautiful grounds which surrounded the Chase, being of the Dutch type, with high close-clipped hedges and wonderful yew trees cut into various fancy shapes. Only old-fashioned and sweet-smelling flowers were planted here, and in the very midst stood an ancient sun-dial.

" It is all very interestin' and pretty," said Dalston, looking round; " very quaint and all that; but what about the arbour, Miss Ernestine?"

" Oh, here is the arbour. Now, isn't this nice?"

She passed in front of him down a wide green alley, and led him into an arbour which was as quaint as it was secluded. Lord Dalston sat down wearily upon one of the rustic seats. " Why, Lord Dalston," cried Ernestine, looking at him with unmitigated surprise, "you are actually yawning! You don't mean to say that you are tired?"

"You forget, Miss Ernestine," he said, meekly, "that I got up in the middle of the night, and I am not used to it."

And this was the young man who had come to the Chase a-wooing, a-wooing a girl who had been brought up in the Shetland Isles, a girl whose head was full of a lover who did not seem to know the meaning of the word fatigue, who would as soon have thought of yawning in her presence as he would of yawning in the presence of his sovereign.

CHAPTER XX.

LATER in the day, Lady Constance and Mrs. Valpé arrived together, and Dalston began to breathe more freely, for he felt that with the advent of other visitors he would be less like a toad under a harrow than he had been during the few hours that he had already been a guest at the Chase. He expressed his satisfaction to Ernestine. " By Jove ! Miss Ernestine," he remarked, " I am glad that Lady Constance has come. She's a sharp woman, knows her way about well. I should think she'd be up to your young sisters."

" I think she rather likes them," said Ernestine, with a laugh.

" But, of course, ladies are more accustomed to bein' under acute observation. I don't suppose Lady Constance will mind in the least having the microscope of a child's mind focussed full upon her. Anyway, I do hope she will prove a more interestin' subject for Honor's observation than myself."

" Honor has been rather rough on you. You interested her, strange to say," returned Ernestine, with a laugh.

218

"Ah, it is all very well to laugh, Miss Ernestine," he rejoined. "I shall be able to laugh, too, when other people go on the grid. For instance, I shall be immensely amused when she sets old Stretton right on every conceivable subject."

But Honor did not set Colonel Stretton right. Strangely enough, the child took rather a dislike to the old soldier, who kept to his military habits of getting up frightfully early in the morning, and of upbraiding everybody who did not appear until breakfast time. Indeed, the very first morning, Colonel Stretton scolded Honor so roundly for not having been out to show him the stables and the gardens that the child was a little frightened of him. Colonel Stretton little knew how well it was for himself that he had thus inspired the young truth-teller with a certain amount of awe. Anyway, such was the case. Where Colonel Stretton was, there, as a general rule, Honor was not, and when she was obliged to be in his presence, as at certain meals, she preferred discreetly holding her tongue to running the risk of having his abrupt, curt, soldierly remarks hurled at her devoted head. Miss Mortimer could hardly understand it, but the relief of finding Honor for the nonce tongue-tied was so great that she was thankful to accept the situation without asking any questions. The effect upon Honor herself was to make her abjectly miserable.

She was a child who had always talked, she had always freely passed her opinion on all and sundry, and to have her chatter stopped at the fountain-head was in effect very much like deliberately stopping the outlet of a well-spring.

It happened on the second afternoon of Colonel Stretton's stay that the whole party went over to a neighbouring place to an entertainment which was something between an afternoon party and a tennis gathering. The younger girls had not been asked, or rather, if the whole truth be told, Miss Mortimer had deftly contrived that they should not be included in the party. "Dear Lady Garrowby," she said, when that lady had half hesitatingly hinted that she had not forgotten the existence of the younger daughters of the house, "I think not this time. I let them go about very freely during the holidays, when the boys were at home, but Crystal is getting a big girl now, almost grown up, in fact, and I don't want her to get into the habit of being seen everywhere before she is introduced. I think it is such a bad plan for a girl as striking-looking as Crystal."

"Oh, yes, you are quite right," said Lady Garrowby. "I am sure that you are quite right. Girls are brought forward far too much nowadays."

"Besides that," Miss Mortimer went on, "it really is essential that they should attend to their lessons as closely as possible. In town, there are so many interruptions, not of gaiety, but of attending their different classes, and mademoiselle and I have agreed that they should work a little harder than usual while they are at the Chase."

It also happened that this very afternoon Miss Mortimer had left a little mission of charity to the hands of the French governess. "Dear mademoiselle," she said, "I know you will do something for me after school is over, won't you?"

"Oh, certainly, Miss Mortimer."

"Well, I want particularly some one to go down to poor old Mrs. Jackson's and to find out what she most wants, and to take her a few little things which the housekeeper will have put ready. You won't mind doing this, will you?"

"Oh, certainly not."

"If you go down in the pony-cart, then you can take everything quite comfortably, and Crystal can stay outside with the pony while you go in and see the old woman. I wouldn't let either of the children go in, mademoiselle. I have never cared to associate children's minds with the everlasting grumbling that old women like Mrs. Jackson seem as if they cannot help. I always like the girls to think of poor old people down in the country as being bright and pleasant and smiling and cheerful, and thankful for their blessings—much better for children's minds. So you will let them stay outside with the pony-cart, won't you?"

To this mademoiselle agreed with most cordial assent. She was a devoted Catholic, Mademoiselle Le Brun, and her private opinion of the English poor would have best expressed itself in a word which is more forcible than polite. When, however, mademoiselle broached the subject of the expedition to the two girls, Honor cried off it. "Oh, no, please, mademoiselle, I don't want to go. Old Mrs. Jackson is such a snuffy old thing, and I have got such an interesting book I want to finish."

"Certainly, my dear child," said mademoiselle, readily, "nobody wants to force you; you are not obliged to go. Then Crystal will go with me?"

"Yes, I will go with pleasure," said Crystal.

"Ah, it's all very well for Crystal," said Honor; "she will drive. I should not mind going, if I could drive."

"You cannot both drive," said mademoiselle.

"No," said Honor. "Oh, I don't grudge Crystal driving a bit; but I have a lovely book, and I would much rather stay at home and read it."

So, soon after four o'clock, mademoiselle and Crystal set off in the pony-cart laden with good things for Mrs. Jackson, who lived at least two miles away. Scarce had they taken the corner which hid the house from view, than Laurence Fitzroy, driving

a high dog-cart, approached the Chase from an opposite direction. The faithful James informed him
that the ladies were at the Chase, but that they had
gone out, he believed, with all the visitors then staying in the house, to an afternoon party at Lady Garrowby's. "But you will put up your cart, sir, won't
you?" he suggested, in his most urbane manner.
"Mademoiselle and the two young ladies are sure to
be in at tea-time; indeed, I believe that Miss Honor
did not go with them. If you will come in, sir, I
will find out for certain."

Fitzroy gave his cart into the hands of his groom,
and followed James into the house. Honor happened to be in the first room in which James looked
for her. She was sitting curled up on a big sofa
near the window, very deep in a book. "Oh, Mr.
Fitzroy!" she exclaimed, flinging the book down and
jumping up, as she caught sight of him, "is that
really you? Why, I thought you had gone away
forever."

"And what made you think I had gone away forever?" he enquired.

"Because you have not been here for—why—it
must be three weeks ago; and, now that you have
come, they are all out, everyone of them. There is
only me left."

"I hear they have all gone over to Lady Garrowby's," he said, if the truth be told, hoping to elicit

some information about Ernestine from her young sister.

"Yes, they have all gone. There are not many people staying here—Lady Constance and Mrs. Valpé and Sir Charles Bonner, Colonel Stretton, and that Lord Dalston."

"Oh, is he here?" he asked, his voice changing as if by magic.

"Yes, he is here," said Honor, in a tone of extreme weariness. "We are not having a good time, somehow. I never speak if I can help it. Colonel Stretton frightens me. He snaps one's head of for nothing. He is a dreadful old man. He is a great friend of Mrs. Valpé's, and they sit together in corners and whisper to each other. I don't know what they want to whisper about. Mademoiselle always tells me that whispering is awfully rude, but it seems to me that grown-up people do awfully rude things when it suits their purpose."

"They do that same," said Laurence Fitzroy, laughing outright at her naïve hit at the truth. "But you don't mean to say that you are really frightened of him?"

"Oh, but I am. Did you ever meet him?"

"No, I never had that honour."

"Well, I wouldn't want it, if I were you. He looks you up and down until you wish anything but that you were standing just where he can see you,

and shouts his remarks at you—oh, it makes my
flesh creep. I am rather fond of Mrs. Valpé, and I
am awfully fond of Lady Constance, she's a dear;
but I shall be glad when Colonel Stretton is gone
away."

" And Dalston, what about him ?" asked Fitzroy,
settling himself down in the other corner of the wide
old sofa.

" Lord Dalston ?" repeated Honor. " Well, to tell
you the truth, I don't think much of Lord Dalston.
He is so silly. He says ' By Jove !' to everything,
and he trots after Ernestine all day long, just like a
little dog."

" Oh, does he, really ?"

The child looked up surprised at some inflection
in the man's tones. " Day and night, indoors and
out, he is always at Ernestine's heels," she continued. " I don't know how she can stand it; he
is such a duffer, you know, Mr. Fitzroy. He can't
play tennis; he never rides; he never shoots; he
won't do anything. Ernestine is learning billiards
out of sheer desperation."

" And does Miss Ernestine like that ?" Fitzroy
enquired.

" Well, I don't know. She never says she doesn't.
I daresay she does it to help auntie. You see,
auntie always says, whatever they are planning to do,
auntie always says, ' And, Ernestine, you will look

after Lord Dalston,' and, of course, Ernestine can't
say that she won't, can she ?"

"Oh, no, certainly not; that would be most impolite.   Perhaps he talks well ?"

"I don't know. It always seems to me as if it
were too much trouble to him to talk at all," the
child said, sapiently.   "As it is, he says meetin' and
shootin' and don't he and ain't it.   I should catch it
hot if I said meetin' and shootin' and don't he and
ain't it."

"Then you don't care about Lord Dalston ?"

"I don't mind him," said Honor; "but he is such
a duffer.   However, he didn't come here to see me;
and if Ernestine is very much bored, well, that is
her business, isn't it ?"

"They have all gone over to Garrowby to-day ?"

"Yes, all of them.   I think it was very mean of
Lady Garrowby not to ask us; but there, they are
so afraid of our telling the truth."

"The truth about what ?"

"About everything.   No, I don't mean in any
one particular instance, but about everything.   It
doesn't do in this world to tell the truth.   Haven't
you found that out already ?"

"No; I can't say that I have."

"Ah, that's because you never tried."

"Well, my dear Honor," said the soldier, suddenly heaving a quick sigh and coming, as it were,

to a realization of the situation, " I don't think that
I ought to be discussing your aunt's guests in this
way. It is exceedingly unmannerly of me. You
must forgive me, and forget that I ever mentioned
any of them."

" But I can't forget," said Honor; " I am one of
those people who never forget anything. Now,
Crystal very often forgets a message or anything
like that when auntie tells her; but I, never."

" I meant it as a figure of speech," said he, wishing devoutly that he had not entered the house at
all. " One sometimes says things that one is sorry
for, and then one asks those who have heard them
to forget that one has said them."

" Oh, well; then I suppose I ought to ask you to
forget that I said Colonel Stretton is a horrid old
thing, and that I was frightened of him."

" Certainly you ought to do so," said Fitzroy,
solemnly.

" Well, I am very sorry that I can't. He *is* horrid,
and I *am* frightened of him, and I should be a hyp-
ocrite if I pretended anything else. Auntie knows,"
she ended, in a tone of conviction.

Now, Fitzroy knew perfectly well that he ought to
steer clear of that particular subject then and forever; but he was young, and he was very much in
love, and he was yearning to know whether Ernestine had been sacrificed or not. " Is Dalston staying

here for long?" he asked, presently, when they had
exhausted the kittens and the puppies and various
other topics of conversation.

"I don't know," replied Honor, with a deep
breath; "but I heard Lady Constance ask auntie
this morning whether anything definite was settled.
I suppose it would be about their going away.
Auntie said, 'No; but I shouldn't wonder if they
came to a distinct understanding while they are over
at Garrowby.' I daresay, when they come back,
they will be able to tell you then."

"Good heavens, child, don't hint at such a thing!
I don't want to know; I ought not to have asked; I
merely said it for something to say," he exclaimed,
jumping up from the broad couch and beginning to
pace up and down the room. "I don't take the
very smallest interest in Dalston's movements; he is
not the kind of man to interest me."

"I shouldn't think that he would interest anybody," rejoined Honor, with a tell-tale wrinkling of
her nose. "At all events, I do hope that they will
have decided that they will very soon all go away
from the Chase."

So he was teaching her billiards, and he trotted
about after her like a little dog, and she was told off
openly to see after his amusement. What could that
mean? Only the one thing, that the sacrifice of the
girl he loved was tacitly, if not openly, an accom-

plished fact. He went on talking to the child, he hardly knew of what, as people do when they are passing through moments of mental anguish. Honor, sharp as she was, perceived nothing. The man was a soldier at heart as well as by his profession, and he pulled himself together then and took his facer like a man.

Then Crystal and mademoiselle returned from their errand of mercy, and mademoiselle, who had more than a fancy for Fitzroy, invited him to share their tea, which he did. More than once the name of Lord Dalston was brought up by one or other of them, always in the sense of his belonging to Ernestine, and at last he declared that he must return, as he had overstayed his welcome already.

" But don't go till they get home," exclaimed Honor.

" Do stay until they come back," added Crystal.

" No, I really cannot, Miss Crystal. It is such a long way home, and I have several guests at dinner, to-night. I can't very well shirk it. Besides, you have your house full, and I should only be a nuisance."

The two girls went off to the stables with him to see his horse put in, and when the trap was ready, they walked round with him to the entrance door that he might bid adieu to mademoiselle.

" Now, when will you come again ?" Honor asked, eagerly.

"Not for some little time. I am going away to-
morrow with a draft of horses for Ireland. That
will take me about three weeks. Then I shall have
a few days' leave, and after that I go to Danford for
a special course of training, after which I shall get
my long leave, so that I shall not see you again for
at least four or five months, if then. Will you tell
Miss Mortimer that I came to bid her adieu and to
thank her for all her hospitality to me during this
summer."

"And when you come back again," cried Honor,
blankly, "we shall not be here."

"Possibly not, but that is the fate of all soldier
people. They are here to-day, gone to-morrow.
They make friends quickly, and they lose them as
easily. Never marry a soldier, my dear little missy;
take my word for it; it is a wretched existence."

Honor looked at him blankly for a minute or two.
"Mr. Fitzroy," she said at last, "what has come to
you? I never saw you anything like this before.
What has happened?"

"I have come to my senses, that is all," he said,
then laughed, by way of putting her keen intelligence
off the scent. "It is just here, child," he went on.
"It always makes me more or less down in the
mouth when I have got to say good-bye to people
who have been kind to me. You have all been very
kind to me, most kind; it has made all the difference

to my summer. I shall probably never see the Chase again, not as a visitor, I mean, because by the time I go back again you will be away; and by the time you are back again, I may be on the other side of the world. Don't take any notice of my blue looks. You will understand them better one day."

She looked at him still in utter mystification, then a new idea dawned upon her mind. "Are you going to be married?" she asked.

He gave a start as the words crossed her lips. "Some day," he said, shortly; "some day."

When he had fairly gone, and the two girls had watched him drive away down the avenue, which was like a glory of brown and gold, Honor tucked her hand within her sister's arm and said wisely, "How queer people are, Crystal."

"I thought he seemed rather unhappy, didn't you?" was Crystal's reply.

"Yes, I did ; but he ought not to be unhappy if he is going to be married."

"Fancy," said Crystal, "his keeping it so dark as that! To be coming here all the summer and never tell us he was engaged to be married! I do call it nasty of him. However, it will be a fine bit of news to tell them when they come home."

CHAPTER XXI.

SOME NEWS MAKES ALL THE DIFFERENCE.

MEANTIME, things were not going very brightly with Ernestine. Lady Garrowby's party was not a very large one, and had, indeed, been got up in impromptu fashion, and was merely the outcome of a dinner at the Chase a couple of nights previously. Like everybody else who knew the Mortimer household, Lady Garrowby was aware of the way in which circumstances were tending for Ernestine. The heir to a marquisate may be as near to qualification for Earlswood as is possible with any young man still allowed to be at large, but he is, all the same, very well able to do one thing, which is to confer distinction upon any young lady to whom he chooses to show attention. That Ernestine Mortimer was likely to be the future Lady Camdentown at once gave her an interest in the eyes of the neighbourhood, which, as her father's daughter, she had not possessed. So at Lady Garrowby's little afternoon entertainment she found herself expected to undertake the task of keeping Lord Dalston fully amused.

They say that a woman always knows when a

man is in love with her, but it is quite certain that
Ernestine had never thought of Lord Dalston in the
light of a possible lover. For one thing, she had
from the very first been in the habit of regarding
him as little better than an imbecile. Her head was
filled with the personality of another and a very different man, and the idea of taking Dalston seriously
had never as yet presented itself to her. She received Lady Garrowby's gentle little hint to take
Lord Dalston through the palm houses with the
good-natured thought floating through her busy
brain that Lady Garrowby found the young earl as
much of a nuisance as most other people, and she
smiled to herself as she thought how completely she
had been turned, willy-nilly, into the position of his
bear leader. Judge, then, of her surprise and dismay,
when, on finding themselves alone together in the
most secluded of a long string of palm houses, Lord
Dalston suddenly began to make love to her.

"You know, Miss Ernestine," he remarked, "you
are an awfully pretty girl."

"Oh, do you think so?" said Ernestine, coolly.

"Yes, by Jove, that I do! And, what is more to
the point, you are awfully fetchin' and *chic*, and all
that, don't you know? I don't know, upon my
soul, when I have met any girl that I admire as much
as I admire you."

Ernestine laughed aloud, a gay, silvery little laugh,

which showed her to be still in absolute ignorance of his real meaning. " am sure I ought to be greatly flattered," she said, with much amusement.

" Well, I don't know about that," said he. " I don't want to flatter you,—far from it. I have always understood flattery to mean somethin' that was false. Now I may be a fool, but falseness was never one of my drawbacks, and, by Jove, when I say that I am desperately in love with you, I mean it."

Ernestine looked at him with something like horror. " *You* desperately in love with *me ?*" she exclaimed. " What a dreadful idea !"

" Dreadful ? By Jove, I don't see anythin' dreadful about it. It is the truth."

" But you are joking; you cannot mean it," she exclaimed, turning and staring at him with wide-open, wondering eyes.

" But I do mean it, of course, I mean it. I am in earnest, I am desperately in earnest. I have never been so much in earnest about anythin' in the whole course of my life. By Jove, do you think I would come here and bore myself in a country-house and put up with the frightful cross-questionin' of a little devil,—I beg your pardon, Miss Ernestine, I didn't mean that, but,—oh, hang it all. how can I prove how deadly in earnest I am ?"

" You can't prove it," said Ernestine; " don't try

to prove it; forget that you ever said such a thing.' Whatever can have put such an idea into your head? Really, Lord Dalston, I didn't think you were brilliantly clever, but I never thought of such nonsense as this. I am sure my aunt will be dreadfully angry."

" No, she won't."

" Well, but your mother and father will be most fearfully angry. Don't ever hint that such an idea ever entered your mind."

" But my mother and your aunt are just delighted to think that there is a chance of anythin' of the kind happenin'."

" What?" cried Ernestine, suddenly realizing how easy the way had been made for this very scene. " Do you mean to say that Lady Camdentown and my aunt have had this in their minds?"

" Why, of course, they have."

" For how long?" she asked.

" Oh, a good while now; since before you came to the Towers."

" Was I taken to the Towers for that?" cried Earnestine.

" Why, of course; what did you think you were taken there for?"

" On a visit, like any other girl," Ernestine flashed out, indignantly. " No, please," seeing that he was about to speak again, and seeing by his face that he was about to make as passionate a declaration as was in him, " no ; don't say another word. It is pre-posterous ; it is out of the question. I have never thought of such a thing ; you must have known that perfectly well. The idea is loathsome, horrible to me. I don't want to marry anybody. I am,—I am going back to the house, now, and I will trust to you to go away from the Chase, and not own up in any way that this conversation has taken place between us."

" But, my dear Miss Ernestine," he said, " your aunt will know perfectly well that I shouldn't go away from the Chase without proposin' to you. I came for that purpose."

" Oh, it is horrible !" cried Ernestine. " It is like sale and barter ; one might as well be put up in an auction ! No, Lord Dalston, believe me that never shall I marry anybody with whom I am not utterly and entirely in love."

" Couldn't you be utterly and entirely in love with me ?" he demanded, pathetically.

" Oh, dear, no," said Ernestine, promptly, some lingering remains of her up-bringing forcing them-selves to the front under the pressure and the excite-ment of the moment. " Let us go back to the house, now, at once. I am very sorry for your disappoint-ment. I am, indeed, Lord Dalston ; but don't, what-ever you do, look as if we had been talking this over. I suppose," she continued, vexedly, "that everybody is just wondering what we are saying, and how we are looking, and what we are doing at this very moment. It is horrible."

She turned and began resolutely retracing her footsteps. Dalston, however, kept pace with her, and did not give up his position without a struggle.

"But I say, Miss Ernestine, don't you think you ought to think it over, you know? Of course, I am not a clever chap, but at the same time I am not a bad sort, and I am awfully fond of you; yes, by Jove, I am. And, after all, I can make you a marchioness."

"I don't want to be a marchioness," said she, without a moment's hesitation.

"No? Don't you?" he rejoined. "Well, you are the first girl I ever met with who didn't, unless she happened to be already a duchess. But that is the reason that I admire you so much and want you so much. A fellow never wants a girl who throws herself at his head."

Ernestine turned and looked at him as she hurried along. If he had had more wit, he would have seen what the look meant, that interpreted it conveyed a question asking could any woman exist in the whole world so degraded, so lost to a sense of her own value, as to throw herself at the head of such a thing as this? Perhaps it was as well, all things considered, that

Lord Dalston was remarkable for dimness of per-
ception. "You won't reconsider it, Miss Ernestine?" he said, just as they regained the outer air.

"Oh, no, Lord Dalston," she replied, impetuously.
"There is nothing to reconsider. I should never
change my mind. Please, don't ever speak of it
again. We can be quite good friends. I don't see
that there is the least need to quarrel, or anything
of that kind."

"You will be a sister to me, I suppose?" he said,
with a dismal attempt at cheerfulness.

"Oh, yes, anything rather than——"

"Than marry me?"

"I would rather not marry you," she said, piteously.

"Well, of course, I don't want you to marry me
against your inclination; that wouldn't suit my book
at all," he replied; "but it will be very awkward for
me if your aunt thinks that I came here on purpose
to propose to you and went away without doin' it."

"But you and auntie surely never hatched this up
between you?" exclaimed Ernestine, coming to a
full stop and confronting him like an accusing angel.
"Did you say anything to auntie about it?"

"No—I didn't exactly say anythin'."

"Then let auntie think that she made a mistake."

"The only thing is," he objected, "that it is the
kind of mistake that, as a rule, people do not make."

"That doesn't matter, believe me, that doesn't matter. I don't in the least mind auntie thinking that you even found out you did not like me," Ernestine cried. "But, of course, if you would rather tell her that you proposed to me and that I said 'No, thank you,' you must please yourself about it. As for your mother, I expect she will never speak to me again. Oh, why did you do this, Lord Dalston? Why did you think of anything so foolish as for you and I to marry one another?"

"I don't know where the foolishness comes in," he replied, ruefully. "And as to my mother not speakin' to you again, that's absurd. You have got a right to your mind like anyone else, just as I have. I am sorry, of course, because, by Jove, I am awfully hard hit, and my mother and your aunt both know it; but there is no need to quarrel over it."

"Well, I hope not," said Ernestine, impatiently. "I cannot think why mothers and aunts and people cannot let marriages alone, and let them come about by themselves instead of interfering and trying to hatch them up. It is a great mistake interfering with girls' marriages. And now let us go back, and do let us try to look as if nothing of this kind had happened."

They succeeded so well, that when the party from the Chase returned home, nobody had the very smallest idea that Lord Dalston had actually made

a definite offer of marriage to the eldest daughter
of the house, still less that she had definitely de-
clined it.

Naturally, the very first news which greeted their
arrival was that Mr. Fitzroy had been on purpose to
bid them adieu. "And, oh, Ernestine, what do you
think?" cried Honor; "what do you think? Mr.
Fitzroy is going to be married."

For a moment Ernestine was too overcome with
astonishment to speak. Miss Mortimer, however,
not being especially interested in Mr. Fitzroy, had
no difficulty in asking the child to tell all that she
knew. "Really? You don't say so? I hope that
you and mademoiselle gave him tea and were hospitable and nice to him, and didn't ask too many
questions."

"Oh, no; we didn't ask too many questions. And,
besides, Mr. Fitzroy never minds how much we tell
the truth," Honor replied; "he is most nice in that
way. Yes, indeed, auntie, we gave him a *sumptious*
tea, and he has left all sorts of pretty messages for
you with Crystal. He came over to thank you for
your hospitality to him during this summer. He
was terribly down in the mouth, quite in the
blues."

"Poor thing! And yet he is going to be married?"

"Yes, he is going to be married. He said," ended

the child in a tone of deep tragedy, "that he should most probably never see the Chase again."

For once, Ernestine was dumb. As a rule, when awkward moments occurred, she was the one who had the presence of mind to come to the rescue and to check Honor's too exuberant tongue. On this occasion, when her deepest anxiety was to hide this unlooked-for wound from the whole world, she had no weapon of words with which to defend herself, with which to screen herself as it were from general observation. She sat quite still, toying with the gloves which she had just taken off, and waiting breathlessly for the next information which might fall from Honor's lips.

"And who is the lady? Did he tell you?" Miss Mortimer enquired.

"No, he didn't say anything about her. He was quite curt and queer, as if he did not want to be asked any questions. I thought he seemed pretty miserable," Honor added. But then Colonel Stretton came into the room, and with a glance of aversion the child instantly betook herself away.

L   *q*

CHAPTER XXII.

It is bad enough for the young when grief comes upon them which is open and fully acknowledged, grief about which there is no secrecy or desire for concealment, but it is much worse when there comes that kind of sorrow which makes those upon whom it has fallen feel that, at all costs and at all hazards, they must keep the fact of its existence strictly to themselves. The news that Laurence Fitzroy was about to be married came upon Ernestine as with the shock of a bomb-shell; yet with it came the great womanly self-protecting instinct that nobody knew her secret, that her secret must be kept a secret, known only to the torn and palpitating heart beating then in slow and dull agony within her.

She braced herself by a great effort as Colonel Stretton entered the room and Honor left it. "Well," she said, swinging her gloves to and fro as idly as she could, "I think we shall all be very late for dinner if we do not go to dress soon," and so she got herself away from what she most dreaded at that moment—the presence of others.

Ever since the young Mortimers had lived with

their aunt, Ernestine had occupied a room by herself. She went out of the drawing-room then as carelessly and quietly as the veriest actress could desire, but once having shut the door behind her, she fled across the hall and up the stairs, never stopping to look behind her until she had reached the safe shelter of her own room. Once there, she turned the key in the lock and sat down at the toilet-table to think over what Honor had told them.

So he was going to be married. That was the reason that he had been to the Chase so little; that was the reason why he had failed her on more than one occasion when he had made other excuses. He was going to be married, he had come to bid them adieu. Well, thank heaven, she had been safely out of the road, and that particular good-bye was a pang which she had missed. Surely, she thought, as she sat there thinking over this new aspect of life, he had cared for her ? She could not have been so deceived. Or had he only been amusing himself, playing with her, passing the time ? It was a bitter thought to suggest itself to a proud nature like hers, it was like a poison which brought with it its own antidote. Some girls would have wept at the sudden shattering of their fondest and most enthusiastic hopes; not so, Ernestine. There were not more than a few precious minutes before her ere her maid would come to dress her for dinner. She could not afford to cry, and, even had the tears been actually in her eyes, the mere suspicion that she had been but a plaything to the man to whom she had given her heart's first love, would have been sufficient to force the scalding drops back again to their fountain-head. After all, she was a Mortimer, and one of her proud old race should never show the white feather. Her world should never know how deep a blow had been dealt her within an hour by the innocent hand of her own sister. If she had been a mere amusement to Fitzroy, the toy of the hour, a plaything who need not be considered, well, he should never know that she had not been playing too. He should never know, nor should anyone else know it either, that what had been play to one had been well-nigh death to the other. After all, her wild thoughts ran, wounds of the heart may be hidden so that none in all the world suspect their existence. Nobody suspected the presence of any wound on her heart, and it only remained for her to be brave and proud to prevent that knowledge being other than her own secret forever.

She rang for her maid, not because it was full time for her to begin dressing for dinner, but solely in order that she might immediately have an audience to play up to. As long as she was alone, she was afraid that her fortitude might give way; so soon as there was another presence near her she would feel the spur of the necessity of controlling herself.

"What will you wear to-night, Miss Ernestine?" the maid asked.

"That pink dress—yes, the one with the black bows—that will do beautifully," Ernestine replied.

She chose a dress of the brightest rose-coloured crape in the hope that some reflection might cast itself upon her cheeks, which, she felt, were as pale as Christmas roses. As she sat before her dressing-table, while the maid brushed and arranged the masses of her fair, luxuriant hair, her mind went back over and over again to the same subject. If only she could keep it secret, if only she could prevent Miss Mortimer and the whole world knowing that she had given her love where it was not especially valued, where, indeed, it had not been valued at all.

Then a new thought suggested itself to her. Supposing, when Miss Mortimer discovered that she had refused Lord Dalston, that she also lighted upon her real reason for doing so? Supposing Miss Mortimer was quick enough to put two and two together, and realized that she had said no to him in order that she might say yes to someone else? Supposing that she hit upon the truth? Where would she be then? How could she deny it? What could she do? In her anxiety to keep her poor, little, pitiful secret to herself, she found herself regretting that she had so answered him. Now, if anyone had told Ernestine an hour previously that the time would come when she would be sorry for having refused Lord Dalston, or anyone like him, she would have declared without hesitation that such a contingency was an absolute impossibility; and yet, there she was, sitting staring at her own white face in the glass and wishing—wishing—with all her heart and soul, that she had known this news about Laurence Fitzroy but half a day earlier.

When her toilet was fully completed, she paused at the long glass let into the door of her wardrobe, and looked at herself earnestly. Yes, she was very pale, her tell-tale cheeks were like a ghost's. She felt that all the world would know as soon as she went down into the drawing-room that something had happened to her, that she was stricken—yes, that she had been stricken a sore blow by a hand not very hard to seek.

" Louise," she said, turning sharply round to the maid, " do I look very pale to-night ?"

" Yes, mademoiselle," the woman replied ; " you look tired."

" I am tired, Louise," she said, in a voice which she tried hard, oh, so hard, to make entirely indifferent ; " that was why I chose this dress. I thought it would give me some of its colour."

" Mademoiselle will be better when she has dined,"
suggested the French woman.

" Ah, yes, dinner will do wonders for me," said
Ernestine, bitterly, as she turned away from the
looking-glass. " There is nothing like dinner," her
thoughts added, " for heart-break."

She found herself next to Dalston at dinner, although he had not been sent in with her, and her
principal feeling towards him was one of gratitude
that he so thoroughly and so conscientiously carried
out the compact which he had made with her during
the afternoon. Nobody would have believed that he
had actually proposed to her during the day and had
been rejected. He talked and made inane little
jokes, laughing at them boisterously, as is the fashion of his kind, and Ernestine, in whom for the
moment pride was more dominant than pain, laughed
and talked and apparently enjoyed herself with quite
unusual glow and vivacity. Once or twice Miss
Mortimer looked down the table and watched the
young couple with a pious feeling of mingled pride
and pleasure which would have astonished both of
them considerably had they been aware of it. She
was genuinely thankful to Providence that everything was falling out apparently as she most wished.
If only she had known that Dalston had been definitely refused, and that Ernestine was sick at
heart and longing only to find herself behind

a locked door in the safe shelter of the friendly
night.

Perhaps it was owing to Ernestine's apparently
radiant spirits that, during the course of the meal, a
little flower of hope began to blossom forth in Lord
Dalston's heart. He had certainly taken her re-
jection as final, but somehow, during the course of
that dinner, he began to think that hope was not
quite at an end ; he began to feel that, perhaps, if he
was patient and persevering, Ernestine might in time
come to see things differently, and, as moment after
moment went by, that little flower of hope grew and
flourished like the mustard seed of the parable, until,
by the time that dessert was placed upon the table,
wedding doves were cooing in the branches ; in other
words, Dalston had made up his mind that he would
not leave the Chase without trying ·his fate once
more. So, having come to a distinct·resolution, he,
not being troubled with anything like shyness, did
not let the grass grow under his feet. He contrived,
before Miss Mortimer gave the signal to rise, to
whisper a question to her. " I say, Miss Ernestine,"
he said, suddenly changing his tone from one of
joke and banter to that of a person who wishes
to be taken seriously, " Did you mean quite all you
said this afternoon ?"

Ernestine looked at him with startled eyes. " Yes,
I think I did."

"Do you mean to say it is all no good, and I haven't got the ghost of a chance—— Oh, hang it all, there goes your aunt! I say, give me a chance of speakin' to you in the drawin'-room."

So Ernestine went off in the wake of the other ladies with a new idea in her mind. After all, if she wanted to hide her heart wound from the world, the way was open to her by which she could do it. Lord Dalston had not taken his refusal as something definite and unalterable. She might be Lady Dalston at once, if she so wished, and, if she were that, nobody would ever dare to say or even to think that she had had so much as a *tendresse* for Laurence Fitzroy. I suppose it would be rude to say that at this point of her career the devil entered into Ernestine Mortimer; at all events, some little imp of mischief came to her that autumn evening and made her as unlike Ernestine, the Ernestine whom we have followed through the pages of this story, as it was possible for the same person to be.

When the gentlemen came from the dining-room, Lord Dalston at once sought for the fair young daughter of the house. To his surprise and disgust she had taken shelter under the wing of Mrs. Valpé, who was the most bright and vivacious woman of the party. Try as he would, he could not get a single word alone with her, although, it must be confessed, she encouraged him in every possible way.

Dalston was more overwhelmingly in love than ever, as he met the gaze of Ernestine's dancing eyes, and noted the brilliant colour upon her hitherto pale cheeks.

At last, just as they were about to separate for the night, he contrived to speak to her. " Miss Ernestine," he said, " I consider you have treated me very badly to-night."

" Oh, no, Lord Dalston, no ! I think I have been most kind to you," was her reply.

" Yes, but you know what I mean. I asked you to let me speak to you, and you stuck yourself down with that old woman and perfectly hedged yourself in. I think you are exceedingly unkind."

" And I," she retorted, " must say that I think you are exceedingly rude. Mrs. Valpé is a charming woman."

" Yes, I know she is, in a general way, but not when she is used as a kind of fortress. Miss Ernestine, I want to ask you a plain question. Am I to fake up a telegram which will take me off to-morrow mornin', or is it any good my stayin' ?"

" I don't know," she replied.

" Shall you mind if I go ?" he asked, desperately.

" Perhaps."

" But surely you must know; you must know your own mind ?"

" No, I don't," she replied, promptly.

"But you did this afternoon, or you seemed to do so."

"This afternoon! Ah, yes, this afternoon; but that is not now, is it?" was Ernestine's answer.

"I shall stay," remarked Lord Dalston, a sudden blaze ot triumph coming into his unlovely eyes.

CHAPTER XXIII.

THE DOUBTFUL ADVANTAGES OF DECEPTION.

WHEN Ernestine found herself safe in her own bedroom with the door locked and her maid dismissed for the night, she sat down to think over what she had done. To all practical intents and purposes, she had committed herself to Lord Dalston, even if she had said nothing. If she had not heard of Fitzroy's coming marriage, she knew perfectly well that she would have so behaved to him during dinner that he would immediately on the arrival of the post-bag the following morning have told her aunt that his visit must come to an end; he would have left the Chase decently and in an ordinary way, and she would have been troubled with him no more. As it was, in her endeavour to hide from all the world the fact that she had received the deepest wound which could be inflicted upon the heart of any man or woman, she had openly and distinctly encouraged him and flirted with him; she had even experienced a certain exhilaration in doing so. On his reaching the drawing-room, she had changed her tactics for those of unscrupulous coquetry. Oh, yes, she knew it, and admitted it freely to herself. Although Ernestine had seen most, if not all, of the disadvantages of the peculiar way in which she and her brothers and sisters had been brought up, and had learned to conform to the ways of the world so far as not to make herself a nuisance to those about her, she yet retained an innate love of the truth. Under no circumstances could Ernestine ever have brought herself to tell a lie, and on this, the blackest night that she had ever passed, she never thought of trying to screen her soul from the actual truth, she never attempted to justify herself to herself. No, she admitted, bluntly, coldly, and unhesitatingly the fact that she had flirted desperately with Dalston in order that she might encompass a particular end of her own, and that afterwards she had coquetted with him as deliberately and as designedly as if she were one of the boldest and basest characters in history.

Well, she gave a great sigh as she sat in front of the glass, resting her chin upon the palm of her hand and her elbow upon the table, staring at her own excited face in the looking-glass and wondering, with a painful sense of confusedness, whether all these things that had happened during the day were really so, or whether they were but fevered dreams of her own heated imagination? She sat long and late that night communing with her own heart. She was very proud, this girl who had been brought

up so differently to the usual way with her class,
and she felt, as she realized that she had missed the
golden dream of her life, that come what might she
would never after this night show the white feather,
even to herself. After all, her thoughts ran, she
had made a mistake. Well, the best are liable to do
that; and she, surely, had not been so much to blame
in the matter as the one better versed in the ways
of the world who had caused her to be so mistaken.
She made up her mind during that terrible vigil that
she would think no more of this gallant soldier
whose business was breaking hearts ; she would live
the life which would please her best friend, Miss
Mortimer; she would let every other consideration
go. Aunt Elinor should be satisfied, and Laurence
Fitzroy should never know the mischief that he
had wrought, the havoc that he had made. She,
poor child, even decided that when they met again—
which, of course, they were sure to do sooner or
later—she would be very pleasant, very gracious,
very friendly towards him ; he should be made to feel
that if he had played a game *pour passer le temps*,
that he had not played at it alone, but that she had
been an adept at the pastime like himself. " It only
shows," the poor child said to herself, " how imprac-
ticable dear father's teaching was. Why, according to his ideas, I should have had no choice now
but to sit down for the rest of my life and tell all the

world that I was heart-broken because a man had amused himself with me! The world is more wise than that, the world covers up aching hearts and bleeding wounds. There is something more noble in the idea of the Spartan boy than of the craven wretch who owns up to his mistakes."

Well, she would begin the new reign of things by going callously to bed as if nothing had happened which could in any sense disturb her. She might sit there all night, staring at herself; what good would that do? It would only let Louise and the housemaids into the secret. No, no, she would get into bed and try hard to go to sleep, to live as if there were no Laurence Fitzroy. After all, a few months ago she had never known this person; why, therefore, should the thought of him break her rest, blanch her cheeks, ruin her life? It was preposterous, and she would not own to such weakness for a single instant. But, alas, it is one thing resolutely to get into bed with the intention of going to sleep, and it is another thing to carry that resolution into effect. No sleep came to Ernestine's blue eyes that night, only one remembrance after another of Laurence Fitzroy's charming manners, his pleasant ways, his melodious voice, and of his lovableness in general. At last she gave up trying to fight against the inevitable, and lay still among her pillows thinking of him as if Honor's news of the previous after-

noon were yet untold. And in the morning she got
up to face a stern reality, to face the fact that Lord
Dalston was still in the house, that he had remained
practically at her bidding and in the expectation of a
favourable answer to his proposal. It was bitter, it
was inevitable, it seemed, in the crude, cold light of
morning, an impossibility that she should accept him,
and yet—yet—what else was she to do? It was a
choice between that and of taking the whole world
into her confidence; it was a choice between that and
of letting Laurence Fitzroy himself know that the
girl he had played with had been hard hit, that what
was play to him had been death to her.

She fully expected to find Lord Dalston already in
the dining-room before her, but he was not there.
Fixed habits are hard to alter, and Lord Dalston had
suffered too severely by his one attempt to conform
to the ways of the house to continue that especial
act of politeness as a regular habit. It was, indeed,
after eleven o'clock ere he sought her out in the
library, where she was listlessly reading the illustrated papers and wondering how many hours of
liberty lay before her.

He closed the door carefully behind him when he
saw that she was there, and came across the room
towards her. "Did you really mean what you said
last night?" he asked, anxiously.

"I don't think I said anything particular," replied

Ernestine, fencing the question, now it had come close at hand.

"Oh, yes, you did, though; come now," he remarked, sitting down very near to her.

" I don't remember," said Ernestine, with a sudden forgetfulness of her principles.

"Don't you? But, by Jove! I do. I remember all you said to me at Lady Garrowby's yesterday afternoon, and last night, when you gave me a hint, my spirits went up to zero."

"Went up to where?" asked Ernestine.

"Up to zero, of course."

"And where had they been before?" she demanded.

"Before? Oh, they had been down as low as my boots," he replied. "May I take it that you say yes?"

"Oh," said Ernestine, "put it off for a little while."

"But I don't want to put it off," he exclaimed. "Why should you want to put it off, if you cared for me as I care for you?"

"I don't," said she, the truth breaking out in spite of her.

"Oh, well, I don't suppose you do as much as I care for you; I don't suppose it for a moment; but, in any case, we may as well get it settled up and let people know. I am sure all these good people in

the house are on tenter-hooks, particularly Miss
Mortimer."

"Very well," said Ernestine, "very well; you can
do as you like about that, Lord Dalston. If you
like to marry me feeling that I really don't care, and
you will never reproach me with it,—because, you
know, these things are not always under our own
control,—why, I will marry you."

"My own darling!" he exclaimed, and was about
to seize her in his arms, when Ernestine slipped
away from him.

"No, no, not now,—when I am more used to it,—
not to-day!" she exclaimed, in a voice which was,
in truth, one of agony. "I am not very well, Lord
Dalston. I am unnerved, and I—I—have had a bad
night. Let me get used to it by degrees."

"You will give me one kiss?"

"Some day!" she exclaimed; "not to-day; oh,
please, not to-day! I have not, you know," she
added, with a pitiful attempt at dignity, "I have
not been accustomed to that kind of thing."

It was not a very satisfactory beginning to an
engagement, that must be admitted; but Dalston,
who was determined to have Ernestine for his wife,
and who was moreover troubled by no particularly
fine feelings so long as he attained to his desires,
lost no time in making the news of the engagement
common property. He never thought of letting the

grass grow under his feet or of allowing Ernestine to get used to the idea of being engaged to him. Oh, dear, no; he went straight away from the library and sought Miss Mortimer, blurting the news out to her without the smallest hesitation or attempt at circumlocution. "Of course, the lawyer fellows will have to arrange about settlements, and all that sort of thing," he ended; "and I take it that we can very safely leave it to them. That my people are delighted at the very idea of my marryin' Ernestine, I feel sure that you know, and for myself——"

Miss Mortimer caught his hand with a little cry. "My dear Lord Dalston," she said, piteously, "you will be very kind to Ernestine?"

"Well, by Jove!" he replied, "what is more to the point is whether Ernestine means to be very kind to me. I am over head and ears in love with her, as you must have known for some time. I say, Miss Mortimer, you will persuade Ernestine to have the weddin' as soon as possible, won't you?"

Something like a qualm passed over Miss Mortimer's soul as the words passed his lips, and yet, in spite of this, she went presently to seek the child whom she loved best among all her brother's children, and when she found her, she caught her in her arms with a warmth and a tenderness which were not wanting in all the finest motherly feelings. "My darling," she exclaimed, "how glad I am!

How proud dear Thomas would have been, your dear father, and even your mother, I am sure, would have been delighted. Tell me that you are happy, darling. You are so young to make such a great marriage; but, dearest, you are well fitted for the position which you will fill."

"Is it quite settled?" asked Ernestine.

"Oh, yes, darling. Surely it was settled when you gave your consent to Lord Dalston?"

"Did I?" said Ernestine.

"Did you, dearest? Surely, you must know. He seems to think so, at any rate."

"I suppose I did," she said, in a bewildered kind of way.

"Poor darling, you are unstrung and unnerved by all this; but, by and by, when things have settled down a little, it will be all very different. I must take you away, dearest, for a little change. We will go to Paris and choose your things. Oh, you will soon get used to being Lady Dalston."

"Oh, not very soon," cried Ernestine; "not very soon. You won't hurry matters, auntie?"

"My dear child, it is not I who will arrange your wedding-day, but you and Lord Dalston himself. He, of course, poor fellow, is most anxious to have as little delay as possible,—that is only natural,—and for my own part, Ernestine dearest, I have always thought long engagements a great mistake."

She gave a great sigh as she spoke, a sigh which told a story in itself, for there had been a dead and gone romance in Miss Mortimer's past, a romance which would have ended in quite a commonplace story but for a delay which had wrought the complete havoc of that part of her life. "I have never believed in long engagements, darling," she said, in a voice tremulous with emotion.

Ernestine's reply was as unexpected as well could be from a young lady who had just secured the match of this season. "Yes, I think you are right, auntie," she said, indifferently; "and, after all, if one has made up one's mind to a certain course, it is no use shilly-shallying. Why," with a little bitter laugh, such as made Miss Mortimer open her eyes wide with amazement, "it is like standing looking at a draught of medicine,—the longer you look at it the more nauseous it becomes. Far better swallow it down and have done with it."

CHAPTER XXIV.

WHAT IS DONE CANNOT BE UNDONE.

IT is a fatally easy thing for a girl to give her consent, no matter how unwilling she may be, to a matrimonial engagement. It seemed to Ernestine, after that interview with her aunt, as if she had almost in the space of a moment sold her soul. Miss Mortimer, naturally enough, being so anxious for the marriage, lost no time in proclaiming the fact of the engagement. Before lunch-time it was announced to the few people staying in the house, and Miss Mortimer had despatched a telegram to inform Lady Camdentown of the great news. The reply messages both from Lord and Lady Camdentown arrived during the course of the meal and were addressed to the bride-elect, to Lord Dalston, and to the lady of the house. Their tone was everything that even the heart of a chaperon could desire, and when Sir Charles Bonner proposed the health and happiness of the bride and groom in a neat little speech, Miss Mortimer looked, as she felt, as if her cup was full to overflowing. As for Dalston, he quite bloomed out under the new state of affairs, made a nice little speech in reply in which he alluded to the grace and beauty of " my future wife," and wound up by hoping that they would all honour them by their presence at the wedding.

And in the midst of it all, Ernestine sat thinking, thinking always of Fitzroy, wondering if he too had been congratulated and toasted, whether he too had made an attempt at a speech, whether he had spoken of his future wife's grace and beauty. She would have been very much astonished had she known what was passing in the minds of the two ladies who were staying at the Chase, Lady Constance and Mrs. Valpé.

" Entirely a marriage of ambition, my dear," said Mrs. Valpé to Lady Constance an hour later, when they were sauntering along the sunlit terrace; " she cares nothing about Dalston. I think he revolts her. It really seems very dreadful for such a mere child to be marrying only from worldly motives. I wonder he doesn't see through it; but, then, he is such a fool."

" It is a great catch for her, of course," said Lady Constance; " but it is equally a catch for him. What a dreadful clown it is! It is like some freak of fate that such a person should be heir to Lord Camden-town."

" Yes, indeed, you are quite right. How extraor-dinary that for once Miss Honor had nothing to say, no remarks to make. Why has that child become so subdued of a sudden ?"

"Oh, my dear, she cannot bear Colonel Stretton."

"You don't say so. Why, what has he done to offend her royal highness ?"

"From what Elinor Mortimer told me, she is afraid of him," said Lady Constance.

"I am sure it is a merciful dispensation of Providence. I shall tell him to be sure to do nothing to remove that impression. All the same, I do wonder that she had not something to say about the engagement."

"She will have," said the other lady, portentously.

Of a truth, the announcement of her sister's engagement to Lord Dalston had come upon Honor as a great shock. She sought out Miss Mortimer when lunch was over and cross-questioned her very closely upon the subject. "Aunt Elinor," she said, "I want to know why did they drink Ernestine's health at luncheon? And why did Sir Charles Bonner and Lord Dalston make speeches ?"

"My dear, you heard what was said," said Miss Mortimer, sweetly. She was in a mood to be as sweet as sugar to the whole world, and felt that, whatever questions Honor asked, no harm could be done by them.

"Yes, auntie, I heard what was said, but I didn't quite take it all in. What did it all mean?"   -

"It means, darling child, that your sister is going to marry Lord Dalston."

"My sister? Do you mean Ernestine?"

"Certainly."

"She is going to marry Lord Dalston? To be Lady Dalston?"

"Yes, dear," said Miss Mortimer, beaming at the very thought of it.

"Ernestine is going to marry Lord Dalston?" cried Honor. "Well, I never did. What is she going to do that for?"

"Because, for one thing, he has asked her," said Miss Mortimer.

"Then is Ernestine going to be mistress of Dalston Towers?"

"Some day," said Miss Mortimer, sweetly.

"Oh, was that why she went to Dalston Towers?"

"Well, dear, not exactly; she went because she was invited like other guests."

"Oh! And you think Ernestine is in love with Lord Dalston?"

"Well, dear, it goes without saying."

"I don't understand what that means," said Honor, with uncompromising plainness.

"Darling child, I wouldn't try. The great thing is that Ernestine has promised to marry Lord Dal-

ston, and she is pleasing herself entirely. You
think, perhaps, because Ernestine is very quiet that
she does not feel much affection for him; but, darling
child, in our class of life it is not considered good
form to make a great display of one's affections. I
think you may safely leave Ernestine to manage her
own affairs. As for you, it will make a great difference to you now and for the rest of your life. In
the first place, you and Crystal will be the principal
bridesmaids; and I have no doubt that Lord Dalston
will give you very charming bouquets and very
charming presents on the occasion of the wedding,
and you will have pretty new dresses, and you will
be very important, indeed. That is all I would
trouble about, if I were you, dearest."

"Oh, I see. Well, I only wanted to know,
auntie, that was all. Yes, I shall like to be Ernestine's bridesmaid, and so will Crystal, I am
quite sure."

But, at the same time, it must be confessed that
Honor was not satisfied with the result of her
questionings. As soon as she was safely outside the
door of her aunt's room, she went off in search of
Ernestine. She was a child who never did things
by halves, and the more she thought about Ernestine, the less did she feel satisfied as to the complete-
ness of her happiness.

She found the door of Ernestine's bedroom tight

fastened against her. " What is it ?" asked a voice, a little impatiently, from within.

" It is I, Honor. I want you particularly," rattling impatiently at the handle.

There was a smothered exclamation from within, then Ernestine flung open the door and asked her curtly enough what she wanted.

" I want to come in ; I want to speak to you most urgently," said Honor.

Ernestine stood aside that she might pass into the room, and turned the key in the lock behind her. " I don't want everybody in here ; I want to be by myself for a little," she said, in reply to Honor's look of enquiry.

" Ernestine," said Honor, " you have been crying ?"

" Well, and if I have, Honor, may I not cry sometimes if it pleases me ?"

" But why should you be pleased to cry ?" exclaimed the child. Then, as she saw the tears well up again to her sister's eyes, she sprang upon her knee and flung her arms around her neck. " Dear, darling Ernestine, I am sure that you are unhappy," she exclaimed.

" No, no, dear, I am not," returned Ernestine, in a choking voice. She hid her face against the child's shoulder and the luxuriant masses of her hair, and for some minutes they sat thus, locked in each other's arms, Honor swaying gently to and fro with that

instinct of motherliness which is deep-rooted in all
feminine things.

Then at last Ernestine burst out. "Honor," she
said, "can you keep a secret?"

"Oh, yes, Ernestine ; I never broke my word in
my life," she replied, almost indignantly.

"Well, Honor," said Ernestine, in a trembling
voice, "it is no use my pretending to you that I am
altogether happy. I am not. I am very, very wretched ;
but it is no use my letting the whole world know
just the truth in this instance ; it can only hurt me ;
people would say that I was silly, ungrateful, and
stupid. So you see when I am downstairs I pretend
that I am happy, and when I am upstairs I can let
myself go and be just as miserable as I like. That
was why I did not want to let you in just now."

"But why do you pretend that you are happy
when you are not, Ernestine?" Honor cried. "You
are not obliged to marry Lord Dalston, are you?"

"Oh, no, dear, not obliged to ; but I may as well.
Auntie wishes it, everybody wishes it. If it will
make him happy and make him better to marry him,
why, I may as well do it."

"It seems to me," said Honor, keeping her arm
tightly about her sister's neck, and pressing her head
hard against Ernestine's brow, ' it seems to me that
it is anything but pleasant to be married. Everybody that I know who gets married seems to be

miserable. I am sure father was heart-broken when mother died—at least, so I have always heard—but the only two people that I have known who are going to be married are both wretched."

"Why, what do you mean?" Ernestine asked, sharply.

"Well, you are wretched; you are here crying when everybody has drunk your health and wished you well, and Lord Dalston says he feels fit to stand on his head with joy."

"Well, perhaps it is only men who feel like that," said Ernestine, giving the first explanation that came into her mind.

"No, no; it is not men who feel like that," cried Honor, promptly. "Mr. Fitzroy is miserable at the idea of being married. I never saw anybody look so unhappy in my life as he did the other day. He looked perfectly miserable; in fact, he wouldn't talk about it at all."

"Then, how did you know?" asked Ernestine.

"Well, I said to him, 'Perhaps you are going to be married?' and he said, ever so shortly, 'Yes, some day—some day.' I couldn't ask him another question."

In an instant the scales had fallen from Ernestine's eyes. "Then," she cried, holding herself away from her young sister, and staring at her with eyes wide open, "then Mr. Fitzroy didn't tell you of his own will ? He only said that in reply to your question ?"

" That was all," said Honor.

" But he only meant some day ? He did not mean that he was really going to be married now ?"

" I don't know," said Honor, who was beginning to feel a little frightened.

" You don't *know* that he is going to be married ?" Ernestine cried.

" No, Ernestine, I don't know. I told you just what he told me. Have I done anything wrong ? Is there any harm done ? Did I misunderstand him ?"

" I am not quite sure," answered Ernestine. " I wish that you had not told me anything. I am afraid, child, that you have broken my heart. But, there, remember, what is done cannot be undone. Do not breathe this to any one of them downstairs. You will make me very unhappy, if you do."

" You don't love Lord Dalston, Ernestine ?"

" No," said Ernestine ; " I don't."

CHAPTER XXV.

THE PLAIN TRUTH IS THE PLAIN TRUTH.

"I WANT you to go now," said Ernestine to her little sister, "and tell any one downstairs who asks for me that I am lying down, that I have got a headache; and remember, Honor, whatever you do, that you are not to repeat one single word of what I have told you to any of them."

"I won't say one word, Ernestine," Honor said.

She had barely reached the hall again before she met Crystal. "Oh, Honor, where have you been? Auntie wants us most particularly. She is going to take us to Rendlesham in the carriage. I don't know where Lady Constance and Mrs. Valpé are going; they are not going with us; they are off on some little jaunt of their own; but auntie says she must go into Rendlesham on most important business—of course, it has something to do with Ernestine—and she is going to take us."

As a matter of fact, Lady Constance and Mrs. Valpé had arranged to go out with Sir Charles Bonner and Colonel Stretton, and Miss Mortimer, having a little household necessity for driving into Rendlesham, which was the nearest town of any

importance to the Chase, conceived the very happy
idea of taking the two younger girls with her, a
plan which would at once combine a little treat for
them with a period of restfulness for Ernestine and
Lord Dalston.

Honor, who was greatly excited by Crystal's news,
rushed away without saying another word to dress
for the expedition. She was, a few minutes later,
returning by way of the great stair to the hall, when
she met Dalston looking extremely disconsolate.
" Where is Ernestine ?" he asked.

" Ernestine ? Oh, I was in her room just now,
Lord Dalston," she replied. " She told me to tell
any one who asked that she had a dreadful headache, and was going to lie down for a little while."

" You don't say so ? Poor darlin'! Then, like a
good child, go back and tell her that when she wants
me, I shall be in the smokin'-room, or somewhere
about the place."

The child turned back instantly, and going again
to Ernestine's door delivered the message, receiving
in repiy the information that she would go downstairs presently. This message she had just given
to Lord Dalston, when Crystal called impatiently,
saying that their aunt was awaiting them and already
in the carriage. So, in great excitement, Honor
rushed off, and was presently bowling away down
the avenue almost forgetful of the unhappy confi-

dence of which she had that afternoon been made
the recipient. It was part of Miss Mortimer's rule
of life that whenever she took the younger girls out
with her she should give them something in the way
of a personal treat. In town, this generally consisted of ices, and when she asked the two girls as
they drew near to Rendlesham what they would
most like for a treat, they simultaneously declared in
favour of ices of vanilla flavour. "You shall have
them, dears," said Miss Mortimer; "but, first, I must
take Crystal into the dentist's just to look at that
tooth."

"Please, I will stay in the carriage," said Honor.

"Very well, dear, you shall stay in the carriage."

So it happened that Honor was left sitting in the
open carriage at the door of the house in the High
Street where the dentist lived. She was well amused,
although she had not much expectation of seeing her
aunt and her sister return in less than at least half
an hour. She sat watching the people go up and
down the narrow street, and presently, to her astonishment, she beheld Laurence Fitzroy, walking
somewhat heavily with a stick. "Why, Mr. Fitzroy!" she exclaimed; "I thought you had gone to
Ireland with a draft of horses?"

"So I was going; but the very day before I unfortunately got my foot trodden on in my own
stable," he replied, stopping and holding out his

s

hand. "And how is the world using you?" he continued.

"The world is using me fairly well," said Honor,
with her most old-fashioned air, "fairly well."

"And everybody at the Chase? I hope they are all
flourishing?" he continued.

"Well, yes; I suppose they are, all except Ernestine. There is nothing very flourishing about Ernestine," Honor replied, with all her truthfulness well
to the front.

"Indeed; and what is the matter with Miss Ernestine?" he enquired. He leaned one elbow upon the
door of the carriage, so that his head was quite near
to hers. The footman, who was looking into an ad-
jacent window, was quite out of ear-shot, and Fitzroy dropped his voice so that the coachman on the
box could not hear anything, either.

"Oh," said Honor, with a long sigh, "Ernestine is very unhappy. She is going to be married."

"To Dalston?" He asked the question in a hard,
cold, set voice.

"Yes, to Lord Dalston. We only knew to-day,
Mr. Fitzroy, and Ernestine is in her room with a bad
headache. She told me I wasn't to tell anybody,
'any of *them*,' she said. You are not one of them,
are you?"

"Oh, dear, no; I am right outside the pale," said

Fitzroy. " But why has she a headache ? How do you know that she is not happy ?"

" Because," said Honor, looking at him mournfully, " she was crying, and she told me she was not happy. She told me that I had broken her heart. I don't know why," the child went on. " I told her the other day that you were going to be married."

" You told her what ?"

" I told her that you told me you were going to be married. You did tell me so."

" My dear child, never."

" Oh, Mr. Fitz—roy ! Why, I asked you myself if you were going to be married, and you said, ' Yes, some day, some day.' I thought you were very snappy about it."

" So I did," a sudden flood of memory coming over him. " And you told your sister that ?"

" Yes, I did."

" And she told you to-day that you had broken her heart ?"

" Yes, but I don't know why, And she told me I wasn't to tell auntie or anybody. I suppose I ought not to have told you."

" Oh, my dear child, don't say that," said Fitzroy, a sudden flood of joy coming into his eyes, " don't say that. It is the best day's work that ever you did in your life, dear child. Don't tell anybody that you have seen me, not even Ernestine herself. I

will tell her. Don't—who is in here?" pointing to
the dentist's door.

"Oh, auntie and Crystal. Crystal is having her
tooth looked at."

"Don't tell them that you saw me; keep it to
yourself. You will? You promise me?"

"Yes, I promise you."

"If all comes out as I think," he went on, hurriedly, "I shall bless you and Ernestine will bless
you all the days of our lives. You say that she is
not happy, although she is engaged to Dalston?"

"She told me that she was wretched," said Honor,
"and she cried, and she said that I had broken her
heart. *I*, who would not vex her for the whole
world."

"I am sure you wouldn't," said he. Then he
released her hand, and, hailing an empty cab that
was passing, jumped into it, and was lost to view.
Honor was puzzled, frightened, and strangely excited. She could not tell what Fitzroy had meant;
it was all as so much mysterious patter to her, and
yet she felt, from the earnest look in the man's eyes,
that he was about to take action of some kind. In
truth, she was burning to tell somebody or other
that she had seen him, but she was a loyal and honourable child, and, having passed her word, would
have died rather than break it, so she was perforce
obliged to restrain her curiosity until she reached

home and could ask Ernestine herself what had happened.

It was just striking the hour of six as the carriage drew up at the principal entrance to the Chase. The faithful James hurried out to meet them. " Mr. Fitzroy is just come, ma'am," he said to Miss Mortimer, "and is most anxious to see you immediately."

" Mr. Fitzroy ? Oh, really," said Miss Mortimer, in a tone of some surprise. " Where is he ?"

" In the library, ma'am."

It was with a strange foreboding of coming ill that Miss Mortimer hurried away to the room which the faithful James had indicated. She found there a scene which was sufficient justification for any presentiment of evil : Ernestine sobbing as if her heart would break, Dalston sitting doggedly upon the end of the great square table on which the literature of the day was accustomed to repose, and Laurence Fitzroy, looking very white and determined, was standing up against the tall carved oak chimney-shelf.

" What has happened, Mr. Fitzroy ? . What are you doing here ? Pray, what has happened ?" cried Miss Mortimer, in an agony of apprehension.

" Well, by Jove! everythin' 's happened," said Dalston, indignantly. " I got engaged to your niece this mornin', and here is another Johnnie turned up."

"Turned up?" cried Miss Mortimer, sharply. "I don't understand. What does this mean?"

"It means, Miss Mortimer," said Fitzroy, speaking very coolly and quietly, "that a great mistake has been made, which has come out in time instead of coming out too late."

"But you are going to be married."

"Pardon me, the little girl—Honor—made a mistake. She took something I said in the most generalizing spirit to mean something quite different; she took what was scarcely even a joke for grim earnest."

"But what has that to do with my niece?"

"Everything," said he, very quietly; "because I love Ernestine and Ernestine loves me. She has offered Lord Dalston to keep her engagement with him if he so wishes. I take it no lady can do more, and many, nay, most, would do less. Ernestine tells me that she distinctly told Lord Dalston, before she consented to an engagement, that she had no love for him. He took her in spite of that. I don't blame him," he said, very gently. "I don't know that I wouldn't have done the same in his place; but if he holds her to her engagement now, he does it in the full knowledge of the fact that Ernestine does not only not love him, but that she does love another man, that man, myself. I am not a rich man, Miss Mortimer; I am not Lord Dalston. I have no title to

offer my wife, but I love her and she loves
me."

"But what will people say?" cried Miss Mortimer,
worldly thoughts coming uppermost as was usual
with her.

"Exactly what I say," chimed in Dalston, indignantly. "What am I to say to people here? You
go telegraphin' off to my father and mother and
gettin' their congratulations; to-morrow it will be in
all the newspapers; and the next thing I have got to
do is to say there ain't a word of truth in it. It's
preposterous!"

"Well," said Ernestine, speaking for the first time,
"you can do as you please. I won't go back from
my word, if you choose to keep me to it."

"Oh, by Jove! no," he exclaimed; "oh, no!
Marryin' a girl who isn't madly in love with a fellow
is one thing, and marryin' a girl who is over head
and ears in love with another Johnnie is quite
another. Oh, no, with all due deference to you, Miss
Mortimer, I ain't as fond of Ernestine as all that comes
to. What I'm thinkin' about is what'll people say?"

"Say that there is no truth in it, that a mistake
has been made," suggested Fitzroy.

"But we cannot explain to the people in the house
that a mistake has been made and that there was no
truth in it," exclaimed Miss Mortimer. "Ernestine
sat at lunch this very day and accepted the congrat-

ulations of the people actually staying in the house,
now, this moment. How can she turn round and
say that she made a mistake? Of course, you
know, Mr. Fitzroy, that my consent is necessary to
Ernestine's marriage?"

"I know nothing of that, Miss Mortimer," said
Fitzroy, earnestly; "and I may say that I care less.
You have invited me to your house; you have yourself sent Ernestine in to dinner with me, to lunch
with me; you couldn't have thought me such an
improper match for her or you wouldn't have made
me as welcome here as you did. I have no fear that
you will try to spoil our happiness by withholding
your consent. Why should you do so? Of course,
I know that I am in the eyes of the world not as
good a match for Ernestine as—as—Dalston; but, if
Ernestine likes me best, surely that should be to you
the highest recommendation of all."

Lord Dalston created some diversion by getting
off the table and crossing the hearth towards Ernestine. "Good-bye," he said, holding out his hand.
"I hope the other Johnnie will make as good a husband to you as I meant to be. It is, as he says,
better to find it out now than afterwards, and, much
as I cared for you, I have no fancy for a wife whose
heart belongs to somebody else. We'll say it was a
mistake; and I think you might wait a bit before you
say anything about another engagement."

When the door had closed behind him, there was for a moment complete silence. It seemed as if no one knew quite what to say; then Fitzroy moved a step nearer to Miss Mortimer. " You won't break Ernestine's heart, will you ?" he said, at last.

" Dear auntie, I have been so unhappy," said Ernestine. " I have cared all along for—for Mr. Fitzroy; and when Honor told me he was going to be married it nearly killed me. I said yes to Dalston because there seemed to be nothing else left to do with my life; and you wished it; all of you seemed to wish it,—you, and Lady Constance, and him, and everybody,—but, now that the truth has come out, you will not make me unhappy by saying ' no,' will you ?"

For a moment Miss Mortimer stood irresolute, looking from one to the other, while the whole time wild thoughts of what people would say kept flitting to and fro across her mind. At first it seemed as if the worldly side would conquer, then a sudden gush of tenderness overcame her, and she put out her arms towards the girl who was her favourite of all the Mortimer children. " No," she said, " I wouldn't cause you a moment's unhappiness for the world, Ernestine. I was in love myself once, but fate was too strong for me. I am not quite what you call an old maid, for I have still a heart left that can sympathize with love. As for you," she went on, looking

24*

at Fitzroy, while the first gleam of amusement that
had crossed her face shone out like the sun upon an
April day, "you had better learn now, once and for
all, the danger of playing fast and loose with your
sisters-in-law.   You mustn't generalize to them;
with them, especially with Honor, the plain truth is
the plain truth, and nothing more nor less."

THE END.

List of Works by JOHN STRANGE WINTER

CAVALRY LIFE.
REGIMENTAL
    LEGENDS.
*BOOTLES' BABY.
*HOUP-LA!
*IN QUARTERS.
*ON MARCH.
ARMY SOCIETY.
*PLUCK.
GARRISON GOSSIP.
*MIGNON'S SECRET.
*THAT IMP.
*MIGNON'S HUSBAND.
A SIEGE BABY.
*CONFESSIONS OF
    A PUBLISHER.
*BOOTLES' CHILDREN.
BEAUTIFUL JIM.
*MY POOR DICK.
*HARVEST.
*A LITTLE FOOL.
*BUTTONS.
MRS BOB.
*DINNA FORGET.
*FERRERS COURT.
*HE WENT FOR A
    SOLDIER.
THE OTHER MAN'S
    WIFE.

*GOOD-BYE.
*LUMLEY THE
    PAINTER.
*MERE LUCK.
ONLY HUMAN.
MY GEOFF.
A SOLDIER'S
    CHILDREN.
*THREE GIRLS.
*THAT MRS SMITH!
AUNT JOHNNIE.
THE SOUL OF THE
    BISHOP.
*A MAN'S MAN.
*RED-COATS.
A SEVENTH CHILD.
A BORN SOLDIER.
*THE STRANGER
    WOMAN.
A BLAMELESS WOMAN.
*THE MAJOR'S
    FAVOURITE.
*PRIVATE TINKER.
A MAGNIFICENT
    YOUNG MAN.
*I MARRIED A WIFE.
*I LOVED HER ONCE.
THE TRUTH-TELLERS.

* One Shilling Novels.

Works by John Strange Winter.

F. V. WHITE & CO., 14 Bedford Street, Strand, W.C.

A MAGNIFICENT YOUNG MAN—*Continued.*

"This is a great improvement on most of the author's previous works. The plot is so good that it is difficult for even the practised novel reader to conjecture what will be the outcome of the mystery which overshadows the life of the heroine. When the explanation is at length supplied, it turns out to be not only possible, but not highly improbable, and is in harmony with the character of the hero. Young Bladensbrook, of Bladensbrook, is indeed magnificent, not only in physique, but in disposition, and altogether a very lovable young fellow."—*Athenæum, August 31, 1895.*

"'A Magnificent Young Man' is as wholesome as bright."—*Black and White, August 10, 1895.*

"'A Magnificent Young Man' is the nickname given to Godfrey Bladensbrook, the hero of John Strange Winter's latest book, and, needless to say, he is an officer. His mother, a well-drawn, many-sided character, looked upon her husband's family as 'a race entirely and distinctly apart from the majority of people.' Godfrey was three years of age when she became a widow, and from the first she treated her son 'as if he were a young king.' The influence on his character and career of having been brought up with this overweening sense of family distinction is the main motive of the story. It leads the young man into some foolish scrapes, but it develops in him so high a sense of responsibility that he accepts voluntary martyrdom rather than allow the family honour to be tarnished. . . . The author weaves the rest of the narrative with so much skill that, until she reveals her secret, we cannot guess at the mystery attending the fate of the hero. The book is one of the best that John Strange Winter has written of late."—*Daily News, September 16, 1895.*

"'A Magnificent Young Man' is a well-told story of modern society. . . . Mrs Stannard weaves her plot with the hand of a skilled worker in fiction, draws her characters clearly, and satisfies the demand for incident."—*Lloyd's News, August 25, 1895.*

"'This is as good a piece of work as John Strange Winter has done for some time. . . . The 'Magnificent Young Man' is cleverly distinguished from a prig. A prig he would inevitably have become in the hands of a writer of less tact. As for the mother, the clever, capable woman, with her unshakable loyalty to her son, who, being a Bladensbrook, cannot err, she is admirably drawn."—*Westminster Gazette, August 29, 1895.*

"Mrs Bladensbrook and her son Godfrey—the magnificent young man—are original and cleverly drawn characters. . . . It is written in the old-fashioned way which the true novel reader loves, without any digressions, bits of fine writing, introduced anecdotes, or descriptions of this or that. The whole book is occupied with telling the story in simple, straightforward style. The plot is hardly probable, but it is quite new, and creates a new set of situations. And both hero and heroine are charming people."—*Literary World, September 13, 1895.*

F. V. WHITE & CO., 14 Bedford Street, Strand, W.C.

ONLY HUMAN.

" ' Only Human ' is a powerful story, true to its title, in that it deals with human passion, human weakness, and human suffering. It strikes an ever-sensitive chord of human sympathy, and is, in every respects worthy of the genial, introspective and versatile author of ' Bootles,' Baby.' "—*Daily Telegraph, April 6, 1892.*

MY GEOFF:
Or, EXPERIENCES OF A LADY HELP.

" A capital tale of society life. . . . The characterisation is extremely good, and, like all the authoress's books, the story is charmingly written."—*Bookseller, July 6, 1892.*

AUNT JOHNNIE.

" John Strange Winter has surpassed herself in 'Aunt Johnnie,' which is as fresh, bright, genial, and one may almost say jovial, a story as anyone would wish to read."—*Academy, June 3, 1893.*

THE SOUL OF THE BISHOP

" The last person from whom we should have expected a religious novel is the writer who signs herself ' John Strange Winter.' But the story proves to be by far the best and most thoughtful piece of work that its writer has yet attempted."—*Standard, November 27, 1893.*
· " A powerful story, quite off the beaten track, and worthy of the fame of the writer."—*Lady's Pictorial, October 14, 1893.*
" We have read few things of the kind that are better than the story of Bishop Netherby's courtship."—*Spectator, November 25, 1893.*
" It is, in our opinion, the best and strongest work she has ever done."—*Glasgow Herald.*

A SEVENTH CHILD.
THE EXPERIENCES OF A CLAIRVOYANTE.

This remarkably successful novel is suggested by the old superstition that the seventh child of a seventh child is gifted with the second-sight.

" It may assuredly be said of the idea on which Mrs Stannard's new novel is based, that, if not true, it is ingeniously imagined and developed. . . . Nancy Reynard, whose uncanny gift causes so many painful disturbances, is made to tell her own story, which she does with a naïve simplicity not unmixed with malice."—*Morning Post, August 18, 1894.*

Works by John Strange Winter.

Small Crown 8vo, Paper Covers, 1s.; Cloth, 1s. 6d.

THE MAJOR'S FAVOURITE.

"In 'The Major's Favourite' John Strange Winter gives us a pendant to her 'Mignon's Secret,' and an exceedingly pleasant, breezy and wholesome little story of army life in the officers' quarters in Chertsey Camp it is. . . . The story works itself out to a happy termination in a consistent and logical manner, and displays the authoress in her best style in a field she has made peculiarly her own."
—*Literary World, April* 26, 1895.

" 'The Major's Favourite' will be everyone's favourite. The authoress is back in her happy hunting-ground of barrack life, or rather, in this case, camp life. . . . The popular authoress has never done better than with these materials. Her motive is ingenious, her characters are charming, and her style distinctive."—*Sheffield Daily Telegraph, June* 20, 1895.

"Not a sequel, but a companion tale or pendant to 'Mignon's Secret.' It is again the tale of a 'barrack bairn,' living in officers' quarters this time, and the writer's endeavour has been to show 'the struggles of a young mind reared with all care and love—struggles between honour and affection, between right and wrong, between a conception of stern duty and the strength of faithful friendship.' In this direction it is entirely successful, and should prove a favourite with Mrs Stannard's many admirers."—*The Newsagent, April* 13, 1895.

"The facile and graceful pen of 'John Strange Winter' has never been employed more attractively than in this story of camp life. . . . It has all the charm of her first sketches of army life."—*Portsmouth Times, May* 4, 1895.

"The charmingly natural dialogue and terse descriptions make the book delightful reading. There are some excellent sketches of character, and the nomadic home life in a soldier's camp is described by a thoroughly well-drilled pen."—*Brighton Examiner, April* 24, 1895.

"The character study of Carmine is well worked out, and her struggles between honour and affection, between right and wrong, between a conception of stern duty and the strength of faithful friendship, are pictured in a manner which must appeal to everyone who has a soft side for children. . . . Simply and gracefully told, the story of 'The Major's Favourite' will repay perusal far more than many novels of a more thrilling character."—*Dundee Courier, May* 20, 1895.

"There have been many books written round a canine hero that have not only amused and entertained, but have also stirred the emotions of sympathy. In 'The Major's Favourite,' John Strange Winter has written a story full of simplicity of style and of interesting incident. There is that blending of vivacity with pathos which makes these stories of hers so eminently readable. It is sure to achieve no less a popularity than its forerunners."—*Colchester Mercury, May* 17, 1895.

F. V. WHITE & CO., 14 Bedford Street, Strand, W.C.

Works by John Strange Winter.

Small Crown 8vo., Paper Covers, 1s. ; Cloth, 1s. 6d.

PRIVATE TINKER.

Profusely Illustrated by FRED PEGRAM, W. D. ALMOND, WARWICK
GOBLE, W. G. R. BROWNE and A. TWIDLE.

"'Private Tinker' contains (besides the spirited and touching tale
of Tinker, with which the book opens) nine short stories, all dealing
one way or another with the love-making of military men. The book
is very light and bright reading, even when the stories are sentimen-
tal ; and, with its happy illustrations and its never-failing high spirits,
is just such a one as everybody wishes to take with him for holiday
reading."— *Scotsman, July* 8, 1895.

"The tales are brightly told, natural, with dialogue that is neither
forced nor dull, with pretty touches of characterisation, and here and
there, as in ' Private Tinker,' a note of true pathos. Altogether the
little volume more than deserves the praise sometimes, but not in this
instance, faintly given—that it is a capital book to take up at odd
moments for one story or more at a time. And beyond that, it is very
easy, if one is in the mood, to read it through without being sated,
inasmuch as the interests in each story are deftly varied."—*National
Observer, September* 21, 1895.

" A collection of ten stories, some military, some civilian, but all
charming, by that most popular of writers, John Strange Winter.
They are united in aim by the legend ' Love Stories,' but the way of
telling these stories has given scope for a variety of ways and manners.
. . . The book is quite worthy of the pen that wrote it. Direct in
diction, truthful in drawing, picturesque in effect, the stories are all
healthy."—*Torquay Times, July* 20, 1895.

" 'Private Tinker' is another set of Mrs Stannard's familiar soldier
stories, and, as usual, full of incident and adventure. All who have
read her other novels should get this."—*Weekly Times and Echo,
July* 14, 1895.

" This is a collection of those charming little incidents the author
knows so well how to portray. Humour and pathos are so touchingly
blended, and her dialogue is always so eminently unstrained and
natural, that one cannot read John Strange Winter without feeling
better for the lesson."—*Brighton Guardian, July* 24, 1895.

"The writings of John Strange Winter need no recommendation
from us—their fame is widespread. Suffice it to say, that 'Private
Tinker' and the other short tales comprised in this volume are quite
up to the usual high standard. Each tale rivals its precedent in
brightness, beauty and pathos, and the whole forms a charming book
with which to beguile a quiet hour."—*Dundee Courier, July* 31, 1895.

" An exceedingly attractive series of love stories from the well-known
pen of John Strange Winter. The short tales sustain the reader's
interest throughout, and are—as is always the case with those penned
by this author—written in a fresh, interesting, and up-to-date style."—
Folkstone Observer, July 13, 1895.

F. V. WHITE & CO., 14 Bedford Street, Strand, W.C.

Works by John Strange Winter.

I MARRIED A WIFE—*Continued.*

whose officers allow social pleasure to absorb more of their time and thoughts than is compatible with zealous care of their men. But nobody, not ignorant or prejudiced, will believe that Mrs Stannard would suggest a military situation without ample warrant in facts." —*Queen, November 9, 1895.*

" Like most of Mrs Stannard's stories it deals with members of the military world, and is a good-natured and very dainty hit at the girls of to-day, with their ' fid-fads,' as the mother of the heroine calls them. It is a fresh and charming little story."—*Dundee Courier, November 13, 1895.*

"Of a vastly interesting and diverting nature."—*Figaro, October 31, 1895.*

"Derrick Lipscombe's experience in the by no means peculiar situation indicated by the title, gives the foundation for this piquant work, in which the champions of ' crushed womanhood,' the advocates of the divided skirt, and overdone philanthropy, come in for keen satire. . . . The work cannot fail to afford the reader much pleasure."—*Sheffield Independent, November 6, 1895.*

"For brightness, and as an antidote to all the humours of life, there is nothing better than a book by John Strange Winter. The kindly playful humour which characterised most of her early books makes a welcome reappearance, and the story runs crisply and pleasingly from cover to cover. Derrick Lipscombe, a manly, straightforward, honest soldier, with just sufficient brains to get comfortably through this not too-exacting world of ours, tells cheerily and directly the story of his wooing of a very charming young lady, a Miss Geraldine Brodie, his winning her, and the earlier chapters of his married life. . . . Bright, picturesque, faithful to life, full of graceful touches, witty, with a kindly humour, this last volume from the pen that wrote of Bootles is worthy to rank with any of its illustrious ancestors—and we cannot give higher praise."—*Torquay Times, November 22, 1895.*

"An amusing satire on young ladies bitten with crazes philanthropic and otherwise."—*Guardian, December 24, 1895.*

"Mrs Stannard in this story adheres to her favourite environment and succeeds, as is always the case, in rivetting the attention of the reader almost from the opening chapter."—*Nottingham Guardian, December 19, 1895.*

" It is one of those shilling books that people buy when they travel by rail—but it is far from being a shilling shocker. The main feature of the story is its restful lack of sensation. It deals with military life and with slumming, and is, of course, well written"—*Hampshire Telegraph, November 6, 1895.*

"'I Married a Wife,' like all John Strange Winter's stories, deals with military life. The courtship of Derrick Lipscombe and Geraldine Brodie, and the subsequent events are told neatly and pleasantly." —*Black and White, November 23, 1895.*

F. V. WHITE & CO., 14 Bedford Street, Strand, W.C.

Works by John Strange Winter.

Small Crown 8vo, Paper Covers, 1s. ; Cloth, 1s. 6d.

I LOVED HER ONCE.

"It is given to few novels to excite such strong feelings—in us at least—as this one. . . . Ingenuity of plot and incident makes it certainly the most interesting, and in its first half the most powerful of all Mrs Stannard's novels for some years past."—*Citizen, April 4,* 1896.

"That the fertile invention of John Strange Winter is not yet exhausted is shown in the new story from her pen, 'I Loved Her Once.' In this pathetic and altogether attractive story we are introduced to a great violinist and are made to participate in sympathy with his early struggles, his sorrows, his triumphant *début*, the desertion by his wife and the opening of a new love which ends, as the reader will see for himself, in a sweet 'too lateness' that will not offend propriety nor gratify sentimentalism. The merit of the story is mainly its faithful portrayal of the artistic side of life."—*Sheffield Daily Telegraph, April 22,* 1896.

"Though but a short story the latest tale of this popular writer at once arrests the reader's attention, and holds it until the last page. . . . Waldemar de Ruysdael, the famous violinist, who is the centre of this short tale, is sketched with power and insight ; and his strange story is one that the reader will not lightly or easily forget."—*Bookseller, April* 1896.

"This little shilling book is most interesting reading, and so realistic is the story that one cannot fail to wonder if it is founded on fact."—*Court Circular, April 25,* 1896.

"A story of considerable dramatic power, told in her best style by this charming writer. The theme is an old one, and the ending particularly sad, but there is so much human nature depicted in the telling that the finish comes all too soon."—*Brighton Guardian, April 15,* 1896.

"The story of the mad dawning of the love, and the pitiful ending of what promised much, is told with a direct force which carries conviction and commands admiration. The story is real, the suffering is real, the characters are real."—*Torquay Times, March* 30, 1896.

"'I Loved Her Once' is such a story as one would expect from the cultured authoress who has long been known as John Strange Winter, and those who have read 'Bootles' Baby' will welcome with friendly interest this latest production from her pen. The story deals with a young German violinist and his struggles for fame in the City of London. . . . The ability with which the story is written is sure to attract attention."—*Dundee Courier, April* 8, 1896.

"The author has described society life successfully, and the incidents of the tale are worked out with skill and effect."—*Nottingham Guardian, April* 7, 1896.

F. V. WHITE & CO., 14 Bedford Street, Strand, W.C.